LITTLE SISTER

Also by Barbara Gowdy

LITTLE
SISTER

BARBARA GOWDY

 TIN HOUSE BOOKS / Portland, Oregon & Brooklyn, New York

Published by Tin House Books, Portland, Oregon, and Brooklyn,
New York

Distributed by W. W. Norton & Company

Library of Congress Cataloging-in-Publication Data

Names: Gowdy, Barbara, author.
Title: Little sister / Barbara Gowdy.
Description: First U.S. edition. | Portland, OR : Tin House Books,
    [2017]
Identifiers: LCCN 2016056178 (print) | LCCN 2017002814
    (ebook) | ISBN 9781941040607 (hardcover : acid-free paper) |
    ISBN 9781941040614
Subjects: LCSH: Psychological fiction. | Domestic fiction.
Classification: LCC PR9199.3.G658 L58 2017 (print) | LCC
PR9199.3.G658
    (ebook) | DDC 813/.54—dc23
LC record available at https://lccn.loc.gov/2016056178

First U.S. edition 2017
Printed in the USA
Interior design by Jakob Vala

www.tinhouse.com

For Antje Kunstmann

WEDNESDAY, JUNE 29, 2005

From her office above the Regal Repertory Theater, Rose Bowan watched a Coke can roll down the sidewalk across the street. It missed the fire hydrant, hit a tree, spun under the café's wrought-iron gate, and set off in an arc around the tables, whose languorously twirling umbrellas somebody had better start lowering.

She called her mother on the landline.

"Hello, darling," Fiona answered over the blare of the television.

"Hi, Mom. I can hardly hear you."

"What?"

"Could you please turn that down?"

"Where did I . . ." The volume dropped. "A special weather statement's coming on."

1

"It's going to pour any minute. Let me come pick you up."

"Wind gusts to sixty kilometers per hour," Fiona said. She was reading. "The greater Toronto area should expect—"

Lightning crackled the line.

"Did you hear that?" Rose asked.

"The day I can't walk five blocks in a bit of weather is the day you can shoot me in the head."

"Have you shut the windows?"

Silence.

"Mom?"

"Do you want to hear a dirty joke?" Fiona said in a changed voice, mischievous and with an Irish accent.

"No," Rose said heavily.

"What happened to the man who fell down the toilet?"

"I might have left my bedroom window open."

"First it got dark."

"Mom, I'll see you later."

"Then it rained."

"Bye for now."

"All right, darling," Fiona said in her normal voice. "See you soon."

There was a long lightning flash, during which the office flickered like an old film. The sound of stately, processional thunder that followed was called brontide, Rose happened to know. She put the phone in its cradle and looked at the Wall of Stars, so named because it was covered in photographs of her father posing next to movie legends. The photograph directly across from her was of him and Groucho Marx smoking cigars, her father seeming to smile straight at her, and it was her habit to look up from time to time and tell him about the theater, its finances and programming, her plans to fix whatever was falling apart beyond the point that it could no longer be ignored. These past few months she also filled him in on her mother's condition.

"She's getting coarse," she said today. "Like a little boy."

He already knew. Today in his eyes she saw the knowledge of everything that had been and was to be, and she turned in her chair and watched the rain.

When she turned back, she found herself reading the plate under the photograph. She blinked, puzzled, and read it again: *Groucho Marx, January 12, 1962*. Her eyes moved along the rows of plates: *Jerry Lewis, July 14, 1966*; *Gloria Swanson, September 15, 1966*; *Mickey Rooney, October 23, 1968*. Normally, even from a few feet away and in good light, she wasn't able to make out those words. But here at her desk, in the gloom, they were perfectly legible.

How could this be?

She looked around the office, and everything—sofa, film canisters, movie posters, bookshelves, the spines of magazines—had the same hyperclarity, and not only that, it was pulsing.

She lifted her glasses. Now black flecks were obstructing her vision, hundreds of them, geometrical flecks like bits of broken lettering. She rubbed her eyes, and the flecks, as if besieged, began organizing themselves into medieval fortresses. Her glasses made no difference. Off or on, the frenzied structures grew.

At their peak, when there was no room left, they collapsed. Rose had a rush of nausea, and then a quick, exquisite sensation of her skin tightening and cooling and her flesh clinging to a vibrant bony web. The sharp vision returned, without the pulsing. She saw a tiny white spider rappelling from the ceiling, its thread and translucent legs. She touched her pen to the thread, and the spider swung behind her desk out of sight.

But it wasn't her desk, her old mahogany davenport. It was a sleek, blond table. All it had on it was a bound document, a laptop, and a pad of paper. Printed across the top of the pad was the word *Goldfinch*. She heard a photocopier going, and people talking in another room.

Her hand, her cold little hand, wrote *Monday, 9:00, Dr. A.* on the pad and underlined it twice. The other hand swiped crumbs from her skirt, which was several inches above her knees, pale yellow, and had a pattern of navy-rimmed polka dots. Her nails were brutally chewed. Her thighs were bare.

The phone rang. She snatched it up. "Harriet here," she said in a croaky, tentative voice that was not Rose's but somehow exactly hers. And the name, Harriet, wasn't hers, of course, but it suited the small, kinetic person she seemed to be inside of.

"Hi," said a man.

"Where are you?" she said.

"My office."

"I'll come down."

"No, don't," he whispered. "Everybody's still here."

She swiveled to face the windows. Beyond a wall of rain were other office towers and the dim stacks of their lit windows. "I thought we had a deal," she said unhappily. "When I call, you pick up."

"I couldn't. I'm really sorry." He sounded sincere.

"It's just, I'm . . ."

"What's going on?"

She shook her head. If she spoke, she would cry.

"Harriet?"

And that was it, it was over. Rose was back at her own desk, in her oak-paneled office. She was wearing her own clothes: blue jeans, a white T-shirt. These were her breasts. These were her thighs, like logs compared to those others.

Her nose bled.

She overreached the Kleenex and had to steer her hand back. An aftermath of misery clung to her, and she let herself cry a bit. She must have fallen asleep, except the precise, mundane details, not just the spider and the skirt but also her cold fingers, her childish grip on the pen, the background noises—that whole ordinary, filled-in world and its myriad sensations—had felt as real as this, only (she looked around) in much clearer focus.

Harriet? Who was Harriet? Rose had never before dreamed that she was someone else. Or inside someone else. Yes, *inside* more accurately described the feeling of visiting, as opposed to having, the woman's body. She sniffed her empty coffee cup and thought of their new employee, Lloyd, the former drug dealer.

He was changing garbage bags in the lobby's two bins. He heard her coming down the stairs and said, "This is the last of the large."

His cigarette-racked gangster voice, she still wasn't used to it. "Check under the sink," she said.

"Okay, will do. Did you enjoy the fireworks?"

She paused. "Fireworks?"

"There was one thunderclap there, I thought we'd been hit."

"We have lightning rods." She resumed her descent. She was aware of holding herself too erectly, like a woman with a jug of water on her head. "My coffee tasted off," she told him, although it hadn't.

"Off how?"

How would amphetamines taste? "Bitter."

"Really? Mine tasted all right. But I take a lot of milk and sugar."

"Metallic," she said.

He spun the bag, tied the ends. "I'll pour myself a cup of black, see what's going on. It might be the coffeemaker."

His nonchalance was so convincing that she felt ludicrous. Why would he have spiked her coffee? What did he have to gain by sending her into a two-minute hallucination? "Has my mother been in?" she asked.

"Not yet."

She went by him to the snack bar and set down the cup. Too close to the edge. Before she could catch it, it fell and smashed. "Oh, God!" she cried.

He trotted, gray ponytail swinging, to the utility closet.

"It just exploded," Rose said to explain her outburst.

"Old china," he said. "It gets brittle."

She watched him shunt around and sweep up the million pieces. Between his belt and T-shirt, his spine knuckled out. He was a wiry, muscled man, still as hard as wood in his midfifties, faded tattoos of snakes and skulls plastering his arm. He always wore the same old rutted cowboy boots, and Rose and her mother wondered if they were the only footwear he owned.

Her mother was the one who'd hired him. Up the street, Terry's video store was going out of business, and when Fiona went in to give Terry her condolences, she found Lloyd stacking DVDs. They started talking. He said he'd been the Strand's projectionist and was looking for work, and she offered him a job on the spot. Four jobs, actually: projectionist, ticket taker, cleaner, handyman. "Everything you've been bellyaching about," she gloated to Rose afterward, as if only hours before she hadn't passionately fought Rose's suggestion that they take on extra help. Under the circumstances Rose shelved her qualms about Lloyd's prison record: eight months for trafficking in amphetamines and marijuana. Anyway, he volunteered the information himself, and it had happened a long time ago, in the late eighties.

"I'll run the vacuum over it," he said now. They stood side by side and inspected the miles of worn brick-red carpet.

"That was my mother's favorite cup," she said.

"They have sort of similar ones for sale at Starbucks," he said. "Probably thicker. And they probably say 'Starbucks' on the bottom."

"She might not notice. But I don't want to start trying to fool her. She's having a hard enough time sorting things out."

"I hadn't noticed."

Rose looked at him. "She didn't tell you, did she."

"Tell me what?"

"She has dementia."

"No way."

"She told me she'd told you."

"Alzheimer's?"

"Vascular dementia." Rose rubbed her face to gather concentration. "You get a series of ministrokes. It amounts to the same thing, in the end."

"Man, I never would have guessed."

"You didn't wonder about her accent coming and going?"

"She isn't Irish?"

"No, she is, but she's been here over fifty years. The thing is, a part of your job, a big part actually, is to keep an eye on her during the shows, and if she starts acting weird to intervene."

He smiled. "That might be why she didn't tell me."

"It's more than you bargained for."

"I'm good with weird." He brushed the shattered cup to the back of the pan. His eyes were also shattered in their way, and yet not despairing. Far from it, when he smiled, he seemed to access a private bliss.

"Well," Rose said, "her lapses are short so far, sometimes only a few seconds. And I'm always right upstairs."

"I'll stop by Starbucks tomorrow," he said. "See what they have."

She no longer suspected him of anything, but when she was back in her office she Googled *methamphetamine*. It was a stimulant, seldom a hallucinogen. She Googled *LSD*, *peyote*, *mescaline*, *magic mushrooms* and learned that they all distorted and smeared your perceptions, they didn't fine-tune them. She scrolled through the sites she'd bookmarked during those hellish days following her mother's diagnosis. Slurred speech? No. A change in vision? Absolutely. Dizziness? Slightly. Headache? No. Confusion? Very slightly. Fear? Not during.

Because of the flecks, she tried *migraine* and read about a phenomenon called silent migraine, where you get visual turbulence and feelings of bodily disorientation and, in severe cases, a nosebleed, but no headache. She kept reading and deep into a clinical study was rewarded with "Some silent-migraine auras escalate and systematize to the extent that they become tantamount to unrestrained states of credible illusion or dreaming."

There it was: the stress she was under had created visual turbulence and body disorientation that had led to a credible dream where she was inside this petite, sad, croaky-voiced businesswoman with really sharp eyesight.

It was twenty past four. A whole hour lost. She was tired, she wanted to take a nap, but she stayed at her desk and returned phone calls. Only when the MGM rep said, "Whoa," about a thunderclap at his end did she become conscious of the storm.

Lightning flared. Her vision sharpened. "I'll call you back," she said.

The stages from the first event came and went: geometric flecks, fortresses, nausea, a sense of her skin shrinking and cooling, of wired flesh clinging to lightweight bones, a wholesale spatial and physical transition as swift and mildly jarring as waking from sleep.

"I'm not cut out for this job," she was saying in a husky voice.

She sat with her feet on the dashboard of a parked car, her skirt up around her hips. Polka-dot skirt, little feet, narrow hips. She was back in the body and mind of the woman, Harriet.

11

"You can't publish two books on the same subject," said the person beside her. He sounded like the man from the phone call.

Rain drummed the roof. They were the only ones on the top level of a parking garage, in a far corner. She wiped her inner thigh with a Kleenex. "Climate change isn't exactly songbird extinction," she said.

"One leads to the other." He stretched. He was a rangy, athletic-looking man with a large, handsome head. "Same problem."

A half-smoked cigarette and a lighter were in the cup holder, and she took them out and got the cigarette going. He lowered their windows a few inches.

"Yeah, well." She sighed. "That's more or less what I told her."

"You're a soft touch."

She smiled, but she was suddenly desolate, and she climbed onto his lap. He had gray, slightly epicanthic eyes. His hair was a rich, animal brown, thinning at the temples. She brushed the stubble that failed to completely cover his acne scars. She held the cigarette to his lips, and he inhaled. They took turns smoking, watching each other, not speaking, and then she tossed the butt and kissed him. It was a luscious kiss, incredibly sexy.

"Now look what you've done," he said about his erection.

Another car drove in from the ramp. "Shit," she said, ducking.

"They're parking near the entrance," he said.

She waited before twisting around. Three women were hurrying toward the stairwell.

"Are they from the office?" he asked.

"I don't think so." She was frightened now, her stomach churned. "We should have gone to the other lot."

"Are you kidding? Lesley parks there."

She looked at him. "When you say her name, I see her, and I can't do this."

"What are you talking about?" His erection softened. "*You* say her name."

"It's different when you say it."

"What time is it?" He checked his watch.

"I wonder what she'd do if she found out."

"Five thirty."

"I wonder what *you'd* do."

"Why are we talking about this?"

She climbed off his lap and flipped down her visor. She fluffed her hair. And right then, without warning, without even a crimp across her vision, Rose was back in her own body. She was at her desk, bleeding onto her computer.

Her fingers overreached the Kleenex box. They clasped and missed, clasped and missed, like the mechanical claw in an arcade game. She guided that arm with her other hand and snagged a tissue. She wiped her nostrils and keyboard and rummaged in her desk drawer for her mirror.

Her face was hers. The face in the visor mirror had belonged to a stranger, a woman about her age, short dark hair, very pretty. The eyes reminded Rose of someone. Who was it? "Oh," she said with a jolt. It was her sister, Ava. She put the mirror away and shifted her thoughts to the man.

Him, she was sure she'd seen before, maybe downstairs in the lobby. Funny that she should dream about the same people and that it should be five thirty and raining both here and outside his car, as if, between dreams, he and the woman had carried on with lives not too far away. She found herself crying weakly, venting the woman's sadness.

The rain had let up. She stood and walked down the corridor to the ladies' and drank water from a tap. A peculiar activity was going on under her skin, all over her body, like threads being drawn. It wasn't unpleasant. She examined herself in the mirror above the sink. She touched her mouth. From what source had she manufactured a kiss she had never come close to experiencing in real life?

"Climate change isn't exactly songbird extinction," she said in the woman's husky voice.

The door banged open. "Who are you talking to?" said her mother with a glance at the stalls.

"Myself," Rose said.

Fiona plunked down her makeup bag on the shelf above the sinks. "And I'm the one supposedly losing her marbles." She patted her hair. Plenty of reddish blond still veined the white, but overall it was getting sparse and required a more vigilant arrangement of the bobby pins that held in place the chignon she wore at work. Snapshots from a half century ago showed recognizably the same crisp, elfin woman in the same uniform-like outfit: low-heeled pumps, a straight gray or navy skirt, a white or pastel blouse.

"So you waited out the rain," Rose said.

"It lasted all of five minutes," Fiona scoffed. She fished a tube of lipstick from her bag. "Wasn't I right about Lloyd? Isn't he a gem?"

"He's pretty great," Rose admitted.

"We pay him a pauper's wage. How does he manage? I told you there's a daughter, didn't I? That he supports?"

"We pay him two fifty above minimum wage," Rose reminded her.

"She's sixteen. She stays with him every other weekend."

15

"You told me."

"Lloyd got the mother pregnant in prison. They weren't married, but they had . . ." She stretched her mouth over her teeth and repaired her lipstick in a few deft swipes. "What do they call those visits they let them have?"

"Conjugal."

"Con-ju-gal," Fiona said, overenunciating to imply that the word was ridiculous and therefore rightly forgettable. She capped the lipstick. "I hope it isn't ratatouille again."

①

Every Monday and Wednesday Rose's boyfriend, Victor, showed up with dinner for the three of them. He got it simmering in a slow cooker before work and ten hours later transferred it to a casserole dish and ferried it by bicycle across the city. He had started doing this after his mother died. He could have joined Fiona and Rose anytime—he didn't need to bring the meal. But the preservatives in the takeout food they ordinarily ate gave him a rash.

Victor was a meteorologist for Environment Canada. From nine to five he issued forecasts, warnings, and advisories. He was good at his job, he'd won an industry award, but he thought himself a writer, and a tortured writer at that. Most of his nights and weekends were given over to

the books he'd been working on for as long as Rose had
known him. One was an encyclopedia of world climates
from the dawn of time. The other, also potentially infinite,
was an almanac of celebrity trivia. Mention any movie
star, living or dead, and there was an excellent chance
Victor could reel off his or her net worth and father's oc-
cupation. Whenever somebody told him he looked like
Paul Simon, he'd say Paul Simon once went by the stage
name Tico, and then he'd ask, "How tall do you think Paul
Simon is?"—his way of pointing out that the physical re-
semblance ended with their heads. Paul Simon was five
foot one, Victor five six. Rose, who was five foot ten, had
been dating Victor several years before she realized that
the pleasure he took in her long limbs was undermined
by the shame he felt toward his own short ones. And yet
he seemed at ease with what, to Rose, should have been
the far more sensitive matter of his lazy eye. Every morning he peered through pinholes in a square of black cardboard, but this, he claimed, was to stave off myopia.

He was forty-four, ten years older than Rose, a serious, steady person, a person of strict routines. But then,
she was much the same. You couldn't be disorganized
or irresponsible and run a theater. They saw each other
Mondays and Wednesdays for dinner, Tuesdays and Fri-
days for late-night sex, and Sundays for brunch and a

first-run movie, unless he wanted to write, in which case she spent the afternoon with friends.

The sex happened at his house. When his mother had been alive, they'd made do on Rose's narrow bed down the hall from Fiona. Now, after closing the theater and driving Fiona home, Rose continued on to Victor's. For several years she'd been faking her orgasms. Trying to have one took too long, while pretending to have one allowed her to settle into the less fraught, more giving end of the business.

She used to sleep over. These days she returned home to be there when her mother woke up. Victor always walked her to her car, although Rose thought if either of them was going to get mugged, it would be him, the little guy with the penlight. Driving off, she saw his forlorn wave in her rearview mirror. He said he understood, and then he telegraphed his disappointment with that wave.

She, on the other hand, was grateful for an excuse not to stay. She didn't like his house. Beyond the dim, cramped rooms, it was tainted by the seedy circumstances of its acquisition, which were that Victor's father had used money from the sale of stolen alexandrite gemstones smuggled over many borders by Victor's mother in what she called "the lady part" of herself. Rose, sleepless in Victor's bed, a bit sore after sex, always thought about the gemstones, how frightened his mother must have been, and then how embarrassed, confessing her "sin," as she called it, to Victor. By the time of this confession Victor's father was dying from kidney failure, and his mother had Parkinson's and an invincible fear that with the house about to be transferred to her name, there would be an inquiry by the bank or the lawyers. Why had there never been a mortgage? How had these impoverished Russian immigrants managed to pay cash?

There was no inquiry. What there was was a widow who, along with Parkinson's, suffered from excessive timidity. Concerned neighbors lifted the letter slot and called her name, and she hid behind the furniture. Whenever Rose came by, she shuffled off to her bedroom. She liked Rose, however, and cast her apologetic smiles. Once, as she escaped, she gestured toward an end table on which she'd left a note that in her shriveled Parkinson's handwriting said, *Rose, please forgive my disappearance acts. You have a smile like an angel.*

Her limbs began to stiffen. Victor fixed her up with a medical-alarm bracelet and a cane, and bought the slow cooker to get dinner going before he left for the office. Late one night while he and Rose were drinking wine and snacking on vintage cheddar cheese at his kitchen table (another of their routines), he said he'd started to research long-term care facilities.

"That's jumping the gun, isn't it?" Rose said.

"You've seen how she drags her leg. She's having difficulty getting in and out of the bathtub."

"What about home care?"

"I like the idea of a facility. They have specialized equipment, for one. They have yoga classes, movie nights, outings to restaurants."

"Victor, she's pathologically shy."

"She'll adapt. She'll have to. It'll do her good." He was cutting his cheese into tiny squares. "Do you have any idea what in-home nursing costs?"

"Borrow against the house."

His response was to get her to look at the websites of places with cringe-making names like Evermore and Goodness. He drew her attention to the smiling residents.

"Don't be cheap about this," Rose said. "It's too important."

His wandering eye slid to the outside corner. "Not everyone inherits a theater."

"That's not fair."

"My point exactly." He shut the computer down and started clearing the table. Neither of them spoke as she put on her coat and let herself out.

She cried herself to sleep. How could she be with a man who put his agoraphobic mother in a nursing home? Over the following days she let his calls go into messaging, and then she played them back and listened to him defending his decisions with arguments such as that his mother didn't like the house and it badly needed repairs and she would have a harder time dealing with workmen than with nurses. One morning the message was that his mother had died in her sleep.

Rose made up with him. He was an orphan now, and her love widened accordingly. He began bringing dinner to the theater. Whether he did this so as not to eat alone every night or to restore himself in Rose's opinion didn't matter to her. They talked about living together in an apartment or condo, making a fresh start.

Six years on, Rose still lived with her mother, and Victor with his mother's fake-wood paneling and high-gloss paint. Unlike Victor, Rose *had* left home. During university she'd shared an apartment with another business major, and during her first year working full-time at the theater she'd rented an apartment above a pet shop that specialized in exotic birds whose squawking and peeping gave her an invigorating sense of living in a jungle tree house. She returned home because her father died. "Don't stay on my account," Fiona said. "I like my own company." If Victor had applied more pressure to move in together, it might have made a difference. But Victor had become devoted to his writing, and Rose to keeping the theater afloat. And Fiona, while still insisting she was fine, so plainly wasn't.

This particular Wednesday, Rose and Lloyd were lugging the heavy stanchions into place and Fiona was clearing out the free-magazine rack when Victor arrived. He and Lloyd had met, and after some initial misgivings Victor had conceded that Lloyd's employment history since serving his jail sentence couldn't be faulted. Even so, he flung troubled glances at the older, taller man, and when Lloyd offered to relieve him of the casserole, he said tersely, "I'm fine."

"What's in it, gold bullion?" Fiona said.

"I filled it too full," Victor said. He relented and held the casserole out. "It's been spilling."

"I've got it," Lloyd said.

Victor eyed the bowl's passage to the kitchen. "The back door was bolted," he told Rose.

"Oh, was it? Sorry."

"You didn't hear me knocking?"

"We were all in here."

He pulled off his helmet with its mounted rearview mirror. He unzipped his orange safety vest and yellow raincoat. A whistle circled his neck, blue neoprene overshoes covered his sneakers. There was nothing new about any of this, but Rose, imagining the whole overwrought package from Lloyd's perspective, was embarrassed, then ashamed of her embarrassment. "Poor Victor," she said and kissed his cheek.

"Was it you who put out that special weather statement?" Fiona asked.

"I okayed it," he said.

"Flooding in low-lying areas," Fiona quoted scornfully. "My shoes didn't even get wet."

"But you always take the high ground," he said, cheering up. He was under the mistaken impression that Fiona enjoyed their bantering exchanges. "I made your favorite," he told her. "Jambalaya."

"I hope you made enough for Lloyd," she said as Lloyd came back into the lobby.

"None for me, thanks, I had a late lunch," Lloyd said. He crossed to the projection booth staircase. They all watched him, this aging, athletic ex-con with his tattoos and ponytail.

The kitchen window was stuck shut. Even Victor, who was strong, couldn't budge it. Rose got a broom handle and wedged open the door to the alley.

"You should open the lobby door as well," said Victor.

"We never leave that door open," said Fiona.

"Go on, Fiona, live recklessly."

"As if I haven't."

Rose let them natter away. She was reviewing the dreams and trying to recapture the weightless, humming feeling of being inside a body so slight and wound up.

Shortly before seven Lloyd popped his head in. Fiona had asked that he put on a suit jacket for the shows, and tonight he wore a blue blazer.

"Don't you look dashing!" she said.

"They're lining up out there."

"I'm coming, I'm coming."

Victor waited until the door swung shut. "What's going on?" he said then. "Are you mad at me or something?"

Rose told him. Not the whole story. Not her paranoid suspicion that Lloyd had slipped her a drug, and nothing about the kiss in the car or the man's erection. "Whoever they were, they'd just had sex," she said and went on to describe her research and her theory.

Trust Victor to have heard of silent migraines. He speculated that sleep apnea might be in the mix as well. "Then again . . ."

"What?"

"It might be narcolepsy."

"Narcolepsy!"

"You dropped off pretty fast."

"I didn't fall over."

"How tired are you lately?"

"I'm tired now. But the falling-asleep part isn't important. It was this feeling of being *inside* another person, this Harriet person, having her flesh and bones, all her physical sensations, but not having any physical control. Or mental control. Like when I was holding the cigarette with her fingers, which had become my fingers, *she* was the one who decided when to inhale and where to look, whatever she did with the body. Do you see what I'm saying? It was like I was wearing her."

"A Harriet suit," he said.

"Exactly. A living Harriet suit, and I was lost in it. I was a thread. A glint."

"You had a dream. We invent our dreams."

"It's just that everything was so solid, so right *there*. Like you're right there, and this table. I could smell things. Have you ever smelled things in your dreams?"

"I'm sure I have."

"I smelled the *car*. I smelled the"—she'd been about to say semen—"*new car* smell."

"Did you notice a digital clock on the dashboard by any chance?"

"Why?"

"One way to tell if you're dreaming is to watch a clock. The minutes don't change. Light switches don't work, either."

"But I wasn't questioning whether or not I was dreaming. I mean, very distantly I figured I must be, but it was like being awake. And what about it happening twice? Twice, I was inside this tiny person with a husky voice like Demi Moore's."

"Really?" He had a crush on Demi Moore.

"Isn't that weird? Isn't it weird that I wore the same clothes and was talking to the same guy?"

"It's called a progressive dream. You pick up where you left off."

"I've never heard of that."

"They're quite common actually. And I don't see any reason why silent migraine dreams can't be progressive. Did you drink a lot of coffee today? Caffeine's a migraine trigger."

"I had two cups." She laid her head on her arms. The lobby tugged at her, the people talking out there, the smell of popcorn.

"Thunderstorms are a trigger, too, come to think of it."

"But in both dreams everything was exactly the same. *Exactly*, right down to the pattern of the skirt." She rubbed her forehead on her folded hands. "That's what you don't seem to get."

"I get it."

"Right down to the cuticles."

"We're going to be hit with more storms tomorrow. The first around three o'clock." He pushed himself up from the table. Wednesday nights he worked on his almanac, and he'd already stayed longer than usual. "You won't want to be driving."

"Oh. You're right."

She helped him into his cycling gear and kissed him on the lips. She waved from the back door until he was out of sight. She was making amends for the kiss in the car, the quiver it still sent through her. If she fell into another dream, would she be inside the woman? She bolted the door, and then she leaned against it and exhaled a breath she felt she'd been holding for hours.

Her mother and Lloyd were talking about pajamas. "I sleep bare naked," Fiona said. "I always have."

Lloyd, sweeping popcorn, said, "Ah!" He seemed unfazed. "Good-sized crowd," he told Rose. "More than I would have thought."

"Henry Fonda brings them out," she said.

"Those blue eyes," said Fiona. "If Henry Fonda had walked in here and asked me to run off with him, I'd have been sorely tempted."

"I'll be down at intermission," Rose said.

In her office she dropped onto the sofa and looked at the photographs. Her father used to bring new subscription members up here and without a shred of modesty, boyish and old-fashioned in his delight, would open his arms and say, "The Wall of Stars!" A mid-1950s shot of Merle Oberon was the oldest, Merle gazing sidelong at his meaty hand on her shoulder. The most recent showed him and Michael Caine toasting each other at an after-hours party for *Without a Clue*. As little girls Rose and Ava had made a game of monitoring the evolution of their father's appearance over the years: the graying of his hair, the arrival of his moustache, the coming and going of his goatee, the unbearable tenure of his leisure suit, which Fiona had thought so elegant.

How chagrined Fiona would have been to think that one day she'd be saying to a man she scarcely knew (*lying* to this man, in fact), "I sleep bare naked." There was a medical word for her descent from ladylike to coarse. *Dis* something.

Disinhibition—that was it. A small victory but stimulating enough to get Rose to her desk, where she took a stab at filling out an epic tax questionnaire. After two pages she switched to watching promotional clips for the cinema chain that employed her as its booking agent.

The dreams scraped at her: the man's erection, the sweet, sweet kiss. She stood and walked around the office, tidying up, filing a few paid invoices. She sorted through a stack of old DVDs and repeated to herself things she had said in the dream: *I thought we had a deal. I'm not cut out for this job. When you say her name, I can't do this.* She scratched her arms and fought to ignore the echoey voices from the movie downstairs. She was tired again, and she lay back down on the sofa and sank into a dead, dreamless sleep. Lloyd changing canisters on the other side of the wall woke her briefly.

The next time she woke, she stumbled to her desk and hauled out her old phone book. She slapped through to the *G*s: Gold, Golden, Goldfarb, Goldfield Plumbing, Goldfinch Publishers.

The offices were closed, not surprisingly, but there was a directory. Rose entered H-A-R, and a man's recorded voice began, "You have reached the office of Harriet Smith, senior editor. To leave a message, press one."

Rose hung up. High static filled her head. I must have heard of her, she told herself. When? Under what circumstances?

"Harriet Smith, Harriet Smith, Harriet Smith," she murmured. Not the faintest image or memory presented itself.

She phoned Victor and left a message, asking him to call. She then redialed Goldfinch's number and got the mailing address: 90 King Street West, Suite 1702. The seventeenth

29

floor sounded right when she remembered looking out the office window. She could go there tomorrow morning. As an excuse, she would bring along her father's unpublished manuscript about the history of the Regal.

His papers were stored in banker's boxes behind the credenza. She found the box that held "Best Seat in the House" and removed the top copy and turned the pages. An ache under her ribs reminded her why she never did this. Every rejection letter had said more or less the same thing: well written, enjoyable, limited market. One time her father neglected to include return postage, and it was Rose, on her way home from the dentist's, who collected the manuscript.

She was composing a letter of introduction to Harriet Smith, Senior Editor, when Victor called. Her news didn't impress him. He said she'd heard the name Harriet Smith on the radio or in the newspaper, a story about Goldfinch: "It's a multinational." He began typing. "Let me just see something. Hypnagogic—"

"What?"

"Hold on a second. Okay, here we go. Hypnagogic hallucinations, otherwise known as lucid dreams, are fifty percent higher among people with sleep apnea and twenty-five percent higher among narcoleptics. But you didn't have lucid dreams."

"I did!"

"You sort of did? But lucid dreamers always know they're dreaming."

"*I* knew I was dreaming."

"They *really* know. Every minute."

"What about lucid dreams where you're inside another person's body?"

"People have those all the time. They dream they're an astronaut—"

"They don't dream they're inside an astronaut's *body*."

"They might."

"But they weren't even *like* dreams. They were so ordinary. Even after I woke up and thought about them, they were ordinary." Another thing struck her: she had felt what Harriet had felt physically and emotionally, but she hadn't thought Harriet's thoughts, at least not on a conscious level. Meanwhile her own thoughts and feelings had been muted, lurking.

"Whether you remember having met Harriet Smith is irrelevant," Victor said. "You heard her name somewhere, and it's slipped your mind."

"It *didn't* slip my mind, obviously."

"You had two silent migraines." It was his job and his nature to conclude based on the facts at hand. "A combination of stress and a change in barometric pressure can trigger prodromal symptoms—visual auras, Technicolor dreams, and so on."

"They were more than Technicolor. I don't even want to call them dreams because then you think you know what I'm talking about."

"Are you saying they were hallucinations?"

"I'm saying they were a whole other *order* of dream." She would call them something else, she decided. Incidents. *Episodes.*

"You've got a lot on your plate," he said. Her mother, he meant. "What are you doing tomorrow?"

"Why?" No way was she going to tell him about going to Goldfinch.

"The first storm will hit close to two. The second, hard to say. I'm calling for five, with a ninety percent probability of both."

"What about tonight?" To have a dream, an *episode*, while Harriet slept. To swim blindly in her emotional drift.

"Clear skies through to midmorning."

After they hung up, she Googled *out-of-body experience* and *astral projection* and learned that for the most part they were different ways of describing the impression of temporarily leaving your body and hanging around as a ghost. She typed *dreaming you are inside someone else* and found dozens of stories about alien abduction, body snatching, and past lives. She Googled the movie *Being John Malkovich*. She'd seen it when it first came out, five or six years ago, but had forgotten the details. A short synopsis read, "Craig enters a door hidden behind a filing cabinet and finds himself in the mind of actor John Malkovich. Craig is able to observe and sense whatever Malkovich does for fifteen minutes before he is ejected."

Well, the observing and sensing were the same, but Craig didn't fall asleep, he got thrown around, and from what Rose could remember he didn't feel John Malkovich's feelings. Anyway, *Being John Malkovich* was fiction.

She shut her eyes against another wave of weariness. She folded her arms and leaned back in her chair.

①

A knock on the door woke her. "It's open!" she called.

"Were you napping?" Fiona said.

"I nodded off," Rose said. Another regular dreamless sleep, not an episode.

Fiona waved at the questionnaire. "You should leave that to what's-his-name. Roger."

Their accountant was George. Close, Rose thought, almost an anagram. "How was the house for *Angry Men*?"

"Twenty-seven." When it came to concession and audience figures, Fiona never hesitated. "Nine seniors, eighteen general admission."

"Not bad."

Fiona went over to the filing cabinets and opened the top drawer. "These are a shambles," she said. Then, all Irish and sprightly, she said, "A man falls down a toilet. First it gets dark—"

"Has Lloyd left?"

"Lloyd?" said Fiona.

"Is he still here?"

Fiona's features strained.

"The guy we hired. Lloyd."

"When?"

"A week and a half ago. Lloyd, you remember. I was just wondering if he'd left."

"Why wouldn't he have?" Fiona said, back to herself. "We don't pay him to lock up." She shut the drawer. "Do you know who he reminds me of?"

Rose put the questionnaire in her briefcase. "I'll do this at home," she said. The nature of her mother's attraction to Lloyd was something else she didn't want to talk about. "Okay." She switched off the air conditioner. "Let's go."

"Crocodile Dundee," Fiona said.

MAY 1982

Rose was dark, Ava fair. Rose big, Ava thin. Rose took after their father, who took after his four maternal uncles, all of them giants with black springy hair, broad faces, and thick glasses that in photographs made their eyes look lost and shrunken at the end of long tunnels. Their father's vision wasn't that poor, and when he reached his full height, nobody considered six foot four to be freakishly tall. At university, where he studied theater arts, he played Lennie in *Of Mice and Men*, and in his Lennie voice he still went around saying, "And *live* off the *fat* of the *land*." Rose, who had yet to see the movie (their mother thought it was too dark for children), nevertheless knew the next line, and in a man's gruff voice would say, "Gotta get some money together first."

She felt lucky to be the daughter who resembled their father. Of course, she could have done without the myopia. It was Ava who inherited their mother's eyesight, along with her freckled complexion and her red hair, although Ava's was several shades lighter, an apricot color. Unlike anyone else in the family, she had green eyes. A fold underneath the lower lids gave her a tired, adult look.

Rose associated this fold with her sister's anxiety about the frailness of the physical world. Ava couldn't watch disaster movies, and despaired of Dorothy's ramshackle house in *The Wizard of Oz* even before the tornado yanked off the windows and doors. She hated dirt, clutter, disorder. If somebody touched her shell collection or her papier-mâché parrot or any of her impeccably cared-for dolls, she waited in silent torment until the person's interest moved on, and then she carefully put the violated item back in place. Not that she was always wringing her hands. She took physical risks. She would climb a tree, and she rode her bike down the steep, winding path to the ravine behind their house. It was the wreckage of beautiful things and the suffering of animals she couldn't bear. She had a terror of tight, enclosed spaces and believed that animals did as well, all animals, right down to insects, so that eventually their father was obliged to release the family goldfish, Goldie, into the Don River.

Their parents were much older than other parents. As their father told the story, they were turning into one of those couples who brag about not contributing to overpopulation, when Fiona's appendix burst. Three months after the surgery, for no known medical reason, she was pregnant with Rose. Five months after giving birth, she was pregnant with Ava. Their father called his girls "The Appendices."

Ava's arrival necessitated a move from their two-bedroom apartment to a three-bedroom bungalow. The bungalow had a finished basement and a fenced-in backyard, lots of space but, Fiona's complaint, no character. She pined after a Victorian house. And then, as time passed, Ava wanted a barn, since Fiona's allergies ruled out keeping dogs or cats indoors.

Throughout these years Fiona held on to her job behind the Regal's snack bar. She took the girls with her to the theater and made sure they spoke softly while the movies played. They became soft-spoken in general and were always being told by their teachers to speak up. Their father was the opposite, a bellower, his so-called stage whisper carrying through the acoustic steel doors into the auditorium. Usually, however, he watched the movie from the projection booth. The girls watched from front-row seats, the first feature, anyway, unless the movie was Adult Accompaniment or Restricted, and then they were sent to the Regal's kitchen. A favorite game was making houses from empty supply boxes and positioning them along roads determined by the floor tiles. Between features their mother or father put them to bed on the office sofa, from which, later, they were carried to the car and home.

One warm June morning a few days before Rose's eleventh birthday, their father drove the family to take a look at ten acres going for a song only an hour and a half north of Toronto. The property included a windmill, a weathered gray barn, and a two-story redbrick Victorian house with a roof like a Quaker's hat. "That's what you call a mansard roof," yelled the real estate agent. They were all yelling to be heard over the wind. Not for nothing was the property called Windy Acres.

"It's like the house in *Psycho*," said Fiona.

"Wait'll you see inside," their father said. "You'll love it."

Fiona loved the high ceilings, the oak wainscoting, and the two fireplaces with their antique wrought-iron spits. But the cracked marble-patterned linoleum on the dining room and kitchen floors, and the layers of peeling wallpaper everywhere, thick as magazines, gave her pause. As did the black ants. "I hope those aren't carpenter ants," she said.

"Just your regular house ants," said the real estate agent. "You can kill them in a day with borax and honey."

"No," said Ava in a small voice.

"No, what?" said their father.

"Don't kill them."

"They're not hurting anybody," said Rose, who lived in terror of Ava's misery.

Their father stroked his hands down his vest. "The ants live," he declared.

"If we buy the place," Fiona said.

They bought the place. The ants lived. On moving day Ava guarded a quivering line between the porch and the refrigerator.

Fiona had hired an old woman who looked like a man to replace her behind the snack bar. If she'd left it to her husband, she told people, he'd have hired a centerfold. She said she intended to become a lady of leisure. But there was no leisure to be had at Windy Acres. The next morning she and the girls got straight to work stripping the living room wallpaper. They taped plastic to the baseboards, and then they sponged the walls and let the soapy water soak through. Theoretically, whole panels should have fallen away. In fact, the pieces were the size of candy wrappers and Fiona had to gouge at them with a scraper. The girls, who didn't have manicures to protect, used their fingernails. Rose relished the prospect of finding money or hidden treasure, whereas it troubled Ava to rip the pretty bluebird-patterned paper, and she winced as if she were peeling dead skin. "Can I go outside?" she finally asked.

"As long as you stay on the property," Fiona said. But she still fretted and after about ten minutes sent Rose to make sure her sister was all right.

Rose walked around the house, calling into the wind, letting it twirl her. She called out over the fields. She went into the barn and called.

"I'm in the loft!" came Ava's voice.

The loft was where a roofing-equipment salesman named Gordon stored his shingles and cedar shakes and rolls of aluminum. In return, Gordon would hire somebody to cut their hay and plow their snow. Their father called Gordon "an odd duck." He said Gordon always wore a hard hat, even in his house.

"He must be bald," Fiona said.

"Does he wear it when he sleeps?" Rose asked.

Their father laughed. "That I couldn't tell you."

"Does he wear it in the bathtub?" Ava cried. "I know! Does he wear it when he washes his hair?"

Since hearing about Gordon's hard hat, Rose had been entertaining Ava with stories about him being an ogre with no skull above his eyebrows, nothing to cover his brains. She described the brains slopping out, and Gordon stuffing them back before his dog bit off the ends. Because they thought brains looked like intestines, Gordon's efforts amounted to recapturing sausage links. "But he makes more in a test tube," Rose said. "He uses worms and his own blood."

Ava screamed. "What else?" she asked between her fingers.

"He strangles people with them. He sleeps with his head in the fridge to keep them fresh."

Ava screamed.

That they had yet to meet the actual man only made the fantasy man more monstrous, and Rose wondered at Ava's entering the barn by herself, especially with all the rusted, broken farm implements pushed against the cobwebbed walls. "Did you climb up?" she yelled from the bottom of the ladder. The rungs, glowing in a skirt of light, were far apart.

"I used the other doors!" Ava called.

Rose went back outside and around to where an earthen ramp led to corrugated metal doors not quite shut. She squeezed into a high, golden space. Up here the wind sounded like somebody blowing across the top of a bottle. Bands of sunlight humped over Gordon's aluminum rolls and made a thatched pattern on the dusty floor. "Hello!" she called.

"There's kittens," said Ava, appearing from behind the shingles. "You have to be quiet."

Rose followed her to a room with low windows, half of them blocked by planks piled at that end. In one corner a tall cupboard leaned. Rose touched its white latch. "This is real ivory," she said, although she was guessing.

Ava knelt at a gap between two collapsed hay bales. Rose joined her and saw the gaunt, filthy mother and her kittens: three orange ones and a white one. The orange ones were nursing. The tiny white one was wriggling the wrong way. Ava picked it up and nosed it into the mother's belly.

"How did you find them?" Rose whispered.

"I followed the mother. You can pet her."

Rose put out her hand. The mother growled, and Rose snatched her hand back.

"Rose won't hurt your babies," Ava said to the mother. "Rose would never hurt anyone."

Rose stood. She told herself that Gordon had changed Ava into a zombie who had lost her fear of dirt and clutter. The real Ava, her corpse, was in the cupboard. Rose went so far as to go over and open the door. Bits of hay, a piece of string. She picked up the string and wound it around her finger.

ⵔ

They named the mother Duchess after the mother cat in the movie *The Aristocats*. Despite an aversion to touching meat, Ava fed her chicken and canned tuna until their father got around to buying a bag of dry food.

The white one, the runt, might not make it, he warned. "That's why animals have litters," he said. "In case one or more don't make it. It's nature's way."

"I don't want nature's way," Ava said.

"That's how it is, honey. There's not much we can do about it."

"We can phone a vet," Ava said.

"They're barn cats," Fiona said. Her parents had raised pigs. This meant—as Rose understood, but Ava might not—that the piglets Fiona loved and named were slaughtered at six months. "Barn cats fend for themselves," she said.

"If they die, they don't fend for themselves," Ava said.

Arrangements were made for a vet to come by the following night.

Ava spent the morning in the loft. Rose spent it flying a purple-and-red box kite her mother had found under the basement stairs. Anyone could have flown a kite on Windy Acres. There might be a lull for a few hours, but mostly the windmill creaked and the grass slithered in long, angled lines. The local crows, Gordon told their father, weighed down their nests with stones.

Rose and Ava saw Gordon for the first time after lunch. They were sharpening Popsicle sticks on the cement patio at the back of the house, making the very knives Rose said they would need to stab him with. Ashen clouds swarmed above the barn. Rose thought she heard thunder, but it was a red truck bumping onto their property.

"That's him," gasped Ava before Rose could squint the yellow blur of the driver's head into a hard hat.

They crouched behind the rotting flower boxes and watched him swing around to the ramp side of the barn, where he got out. He was a short, wide man in blue overalls. He climbed the ramp, yanked apart the doors, and entered.

"I hope he doesn't scare Duchess," Ava said.

They waited. After only a few minutes they heard yelling.

"What's the matter?" Ava cried.

A black cat flew down the ramp. Then Gordon bar-reled down, waving a shovel. "Go on, scram!" he yelled. He banged the shovel on the flatbed of his truck, and the cat took off into the mustard field.

Fiona was already out the screen door. She and the girls ran to Gordon, who had dropped the shovel and was studying a gash on his forearm. His arms were chubby and hairless, his face the same. Rose couldn't tell adults' ages, but he was clearly a lot younger than the hoary maniac she'd invented.

"What happened?" their mother said.

"Ah, I couldn't grab him." He looked at Ava and Rose before saying, "He got the kittens."

"Stay put," Fiona ordered the girls, and she followed Gordon into the barn.

"What does he mean, *got*?" Ava said.

"I'm not sure," Rose lied.

"I think he means killed."

"I'm not sure."

Ava sat on the ground.

"It's dirty there!" Rose cried. She saw obscenity in the splay of her sister's legs. Thunder roared, real thunder. Fiona and Gordon returned, Fiona with the kittens in her apron. Rose demanded to look. There was no blood,

45

but the limpness, the lifelessness, was unmistakable. She asked why the black cat had killed them.

"They wasn't his," Gordon answered. "He gave 'em a shake, and that was it. Wouldn't a hurt at all."

"Get up, darling," Fiona said to Ava.

"What about Duchess?" Rose asked.

"She. . ." Fiona looked at Gordon.

"You mean the mother?" he said.

Rose nodded.

"He chased her off. I seen her get away." From his back pocket he tugged a large gray handkerchief and tied it around his wound. "Here comes the rain."

"Ava, darling, we'll give them a nice burial. Get up now."

Ava shook her head.

Gordon scooped Ava into his arms. Rose expected her to protest, but she stayed folded like a lawn chair, and they all ran for the house.

He lowered Ava onto the porch sofa. He called her Red: "There we go, Red." He brushed dirt from her bare thighs and from beneath the hem of her shorts. Fiona, occupied as she was opening the kitchen door, didn't notice. Rose noticed.

"I want to clean that cut," Fiona said. "I won't be a minute."

She went into the house. Gordon pulled the string on the bare lightbulb. It reflected minutely in his hard hat, as if he had an idea. Rain pelted the metal shingles. Rose sat, turned away from him, and brushed her sister's legs herself.

"You put some food out," he said, "the mother might come back."

THURSDAY, JUNE 30, 2005

Rose slept soundly and dreamlessly until her mother jostled her shoulder and said, "It's twenty to eight. The breakfast room's closing."

About two mornings a week Fiona got dressed in white sailor pants and a green-and-white-striped jersey and set about exploring the cruise ship she believed herself to be on. Notes taped to the fridge and bathroom mirror, saying, *FIONA—YOU ARE AT HOME IN YOUR HOUSE*, sometimes snapped her out of it. Not today, obviously.

"It's me," Rose said. "Rose."

"Where's your father?"

"Mom, he died."

"He didn't die."

"He did. Nine years ago."

Fiona peered around as if for her purse or the exit. "I want to go home."

"You *are* home," Rose said. "In your house on Millwood Avenue." She got up and went to the window and threw back the drapes.

The sky was hazy. The grass steamed. She opened the drapes wider to bring their bird feeder into view. "The thugs are back," she said.

Fiona joined her, and they watched two grackles fling seed. Clumped along the power lines, a dozen sparrows waited in silence.

"Song sparrows are your favorite," Fiona said.

"I think those are chipping sparrows," Rose said. She didn't have her glasses on.

"Chipping sparrows," said Fiona. Her face showed an intensity of thought.

"There might be one song sparrow," Rose allowed.

"Mother of God," said Fiona in her regular voice. "I've done it again, haven't I?"

"You should actually go on a cruise," Rose said.

"And hire somebody to toss me overboard. I'm sorry, Rose. Can you get back to sleep?"

"I'll stay up. I'm seeing George, so I may as well make an early start."

In the shower Rose decided that she *would* see their accountant. For the sake of not lying to her mother, and to get help with the tax questionnaire, she would drop by his office after her visit to Goldfinch Publishers.

Naturally she wanted to see if the Harriet from her episodes was anything like the real-life Harriet. She was more than curious, though, she was compelled, and she didn't understand exactly why. What she told herself was that the real-life Harriet would spark a memory, a recognition, and in a way not yet clear to her, the episodes would make sense.

She set out on foot shortly before nine thirty. Downtown was no great distance, three or four miles, and she felt she needed the exercise and extra time to marshal her nerve. She crossed the park and headed south to Davisville Avenue, a little astonished that she was going through with this, she who had a dread of drawing attention to herself.

And yet here she was, hoping to lie her way into Harriet's presence, and not only that, she was wearing a loud turquoise-and-orange, Indian-patterned dress, ankle-length, flowing, something she had bought years ago and never until this morning taken off the hanger. It was the kind of dress she imagined a writer, or the daughter of a writer, wearing. She would breeze into

Goldfinch and say, "I'm here to see Harriet Smith." The receptionist would ask for a name, then check with Harriet, who (this only now occurred to Rose) might not be inclined to come out and talk to a person she didn't know. In that case, Rose would say, "I have a manuscript for her. I just need to tell her a few things about it first." She rehearsed these phrases in her mind. She walked more aggressively.

It was hot, and as much as possible she kept to the shade. But there was no escaping the humidity, and by Yonge Street she was soaked with sweat. She hailed a cab. In the backseat she fished Kleenex from the bottom of her purse and dried under her arms.

The driver maneuvered his mirror to see her better. He had a pretty pink mouth and plump cheeks. She wondered if he wasn't actually a woman until he spoke. "Are you married?" he asked.

His soft features somehow divested the question of intrusiveness. "No," she said, "not married."

"Do you make a good living?"

"I get by."

"If you were my woman, I would lift weights all day so that when you came home from work I could make love to you all night."

"I'm in a relationship."

He reached over his seat and handed her a card. She tried to give it back but he said, "Give it to one of your girlfriends who makes a good living."

Many of the office towers in this part of town were glass. It was not amazing, therefore, that Harriet's should be. And yet Rose *was* amazed. In a state far more dream-like than the episodes, she entered the lobby and took the elevator up to the seventeenth floor. The doors opened onto a mahogany-paneled reception area. This, too, was dreamlike: the absence of an intervening corridor.

The receptionist stood, not to greet Rose, rather to start sawing open a cardboard box. "Good morning, Goldfinch Publishers," she said into her mouthpiece, halting Rose with a tilt of her knife. Her hair was pulled back tight, and she had the lean features and severely arched eyebrows Rose associated with women not easily charmed.

The call dragged on. Rose crossed to a wall of photographs, the largest a blown-up newspaper clipping. *Birds of a Feather Flock Together*, she read. *Vireo Press and Cardinal Publishers join forces to create Goldfinch.*

Vireo and Cardinal were familiar, especially Cardinal and its red paperbacks. Rose looked around, and now everything was familiar enough for her to conclude that these were the old Cardinal offices and that she had collected her father's manuscript—the manuscript she carried with her—from this very place, although too long ago for Harriet to have been here.

"May I help you?" said the receptionist.

Rose swung around. "Oh, hi." She stepped closer. "I'm here to see Harriet Smith."

"Reception," said the receptionist and turned to her computer screen. A narrow braid, like a zipper, bisected the back of her skull. "Tomorrow at noon," she said. Then, "She isn't in today."

It took a moment for Rose to understand that this second statement was meant for her. "Harriet isn't in?"

"She's working from home."

"But we had an appointment."

"She isn't here, I'm afraid."

"I have a manuscript for her," Rose said.

The receptionist pointed her knife at a coffee table already piled with padded envelopes. "You can leave it there."

Rose considered. Although Harriet wasn't in, her boyfriend, the man from the car, might be. "May I use your washroom?" she asked.

"They have a washroom in the ground-floor coffee shop."

"It's a bit of an emergency."

The receptionist eyed Rose's body, as if the emergency

were connected to her flashy dress. "Through that door," she said. A curt nod. "All the way to the end."

All the way to the end was a long way. On either side were identical offices, the windowless ones scarcely bigger than their desks. Nobody glanced up. She passed the washrooms, rounded the corner, and kept going. Ahead of her a man and woman were in conversation. "Keyless entry," said the woman, "push-button start."

"Sorry," Rose said.

They shifted to let her by. "Rear-seat DVD," the woman resumed.

The next office was unoccupied. The office after that was not.

He stood at the window. From his back, she knew him.

He turned. "Looking for me?" he said, smiling.

"No, I . . . no," she stammered. "I was . . . Is the washroom?"

"End of the hall." He pointed the way she'd come. "Hang a left."

"Thank you." But she couldn't bring herself to move.

The long, angled eyes ransacked her face. "Anything else I can help you with?"

"No, sorry." Thermal waves pulsed from Rose's midriff. "I just . . . have you ever been to the Regal Theater up on Mount Pleasant?"

"The Regal? Sure. Not lately, but yeah."

"Okay." Her face, she knew, was flaming. "I thought I'd seen you before."

"Do you go there a lot?"

"Actually, I own it. With my mother."

"You own that gorgeous building?"

"Well, the bank does."

He came closer and extended his hand. "David Novak."

Her hand in his felt like mush, as if he had pressed a nerve that collapsed her joints. "Rose Bowan."

"I love the, what do you call it, the dome."

"The cupola."

"Cupola. Right. It's spectacular."

Should she mention Harriet? If he offered to give Harriet the manuscript, would that help Rose meet her in person? Probably the receptionist was wondering what was taking her so long. "So the washroom . . . ?"

"End of that hall, turn left."

"Thank you."

"No problem."

Back she went, as fast as her rubbery legs would carry her, past the washrooms, through the reception area, and across to the open elevator.

At one of the coffee shop's window tables she drank iced tea. She would come back tomorrow. Or, no, tomorrow was a holiday—she would have to wait until Monday. She would show up early, before eight, stand at the ground-floor elevators and catch Harriet arriving for work.

Had she ever been this turned on in her life? She had, yesterday, straddling David's lap, or rather her fantasized version of his lap. This arousal wasn't strictly hers then, it was contact arousal, generated by Harriet. Who also happened to be a fantasized version. So, really, the arousal was Rose's, but for reasons she didn't need years of therapy to identify, although those years were there, she could access it only through a made-up woman based on a real woman she'd forgotten ever having laid eyes on.

Straightforward truths *did* exist, she reminded herself. David, for example. The Goldfinch reception area.

Suppose she had asked David what kind of car he drove, and he said a Camry, and she Googled *Camry*, and there was the car interior from her second episode? How would she account for it? She'd have to think: I was in a Camry once and remembered the dashboard, even though I have no interest in cars and no memory of the occasion itself. Or: I'm making things up as I go along. I see a car online and alter my perceptions accordingly.

Sort of like how a stroke victim thinks.

She allowed the analogy because she didn't really believe it. Her mind was too available to her, too aware of itself. She leaned closer to the window and peered up. From what she could see, the sky was mostly blue, but the wind had risen. Her heart pounded. Forget it, she told herself. Even if the storm brought on another episode, the odds that she would enter Harriet and encounter David—David as he'd just been, Harriet similarly unmorphed, the pair of them following to the letter their earlier narrative—were astronomical.

Forget it.

So she forgot it. She was accustomed to keeping her hopes low. On the subway she read the tax questionnaire. At her accountant's office she paid close attention to the Regal's humble investment portfolio. Afterward, taking a taxi back to the theater, she listened to messages on her cell.

The first was from Victor, an abrupt, "Hi, give me a call." The last, from Fiona, was an ominous, "He's out there."

Rose phoned her mother. "*Who's* out there?"

"The old man. What's-his-name."

"Charles?"

"He's on his porch."

"So?"

"He's leering at me."

Charles lived across the street. He was an eighty-five-year-old former government chauffeur from Kenya. This past December he'd arrived in Canada to live out his days with Caroline, the youngest of his grandchildren. He'd stayed indoors until spring, and then he'd taken up residence for hours at a time on the porch sofa, a tall, straight, pole-limbed man wearing a light blue or gray three-piece suit, motionless apart from the levering of his right arm as he brought a cigarette to his lips.

"He probably can't even see you," Rose said, watching the sky. The streamers were sailing in. "You're probably a blur."

"He's waiting for me to bend over. They're like dogs that way."

Rose hung her head. By "they," she devoutly hoped her mother meant old men, not black men. Old people had a right to find each other repellent.

"I want you to talk to Caroline," Fiona said.

"It isn't his fault if he can't take his eyes off you."

"He's gone through four wives."

"Mom, do something out back. I've got to go."

"Well, *you* phoned *me*."

She called Victor next.

"You had Chinese for lunch yesterday," he said. "Right?"

"Yeah."

"MSG. Major migraine trigger."

"Wang's doesn't use MSG."

"Are you sure?"

"Not really." She reached to pay the driver. "So around two o'clock for the storm?"

"More like two fifteen, two thirty. I'm betting it's MSG, but let me know."

Several girls from the nearby private school were discussing the COMING SOON poster of Marilyn Monroe in *Bus Stop*. "They're like *my* legs," one of them said, flipping her skirt, and Rose, walking past, saw that it was the same skirt as Harriet's, exactly the same: pale yellow with dime-sized, navy-rimmed polka dots.

An effervescent tension started up behind her eyes. It seemed connected to the polka dots. Was she about to have an episode? She frantically sorted through her keys while resisting an impulse to ask the girl where she'd bought the skirt. As if that would tell her anything.

The tension vanished the moment she was inside. She went over to the staircase and sat on a step and kicked off her sandals. Her encounter with David, her mother's hateful paranoia, the heat, the skirt. All this was taking a toll.

She looked around the lobby, never at its best with daylight streaming through the glass doors. The widest cracks in the plaster Lloyd was beginning to repair. The carpet needed replacing, but he said he could hide the rips with duct tape on the underside.

Her parents had laid this carpet, just the two of them. One of Rose's first memories was of her mother on her hands and knees, and the raw sound of her scissors cutting through the nylon pile. The original carpet went down twenty years before that, during the theater's massive overhaul. In those days, the early fifties, it belonged to Ricky Renaldo, and Rose's father did little more than fly to New York City to meet with Ricky's decorators and suppliers. Back in Toronto he was required to turn up at boozy lunches and listen to Ricky reminisce about the musicians and actors he'd rescued from poverty. Where had Ricky's money come from? Investments, Ricky said. *Crooked, offshore* investments, her father heard. Whatever the source, it ran out a month before the grand opening. As uniformed men hired by Ricky's creditors were carrying out the lobby furniture, Ricky was driving his Cadillac at high speed into a cement embankment.

Rose's father was too stunned to see his opportunity. Not so his bride. On the day of the funeral Fiona talked her uncle into cosigning a loan that enabled the newlyweds to buy the restored former vaudevillian theater where, as a child, Rose's father had watched a man in a rabbit costume jump through hoops of fire.

Seldom did Rose think of those days, the heydays, before she and Ava were born. Normally when she thought about them, she was at home in bed, unable to sleep, worrying about money. This morning on the stairs, facing the vestibule and the retired box office with its gothic windows she otherwise never noticed, she marveled at her parents' courage and faith in buying the theater and then making the risky decision to show second runs and classics. Her mother claimed that she had never doubted they would make a go of it. "Your father was a zealot," she said.

Rose was not a zealot. Rose lacked the single-mindedness and other necessary qualities, such as joy in mingling with the patrons (quizzing them, soliciting their opinions, offering men cigars after a screening of *Dr. Strangelove*) and the passion and gall it takes to insinuate yourself into exclusive publicity parties. Zealotry dies with the zealot. In that, Rose suspected, it was like genius, and she was like Frank Sinatra Jr. and Liza Minnelli. Even her extra job booking films for DeLux had come about through her father's connections.

But Rose knew herself to be lucky. This theater, this work, getting to screen great movies day after day and having people tell you how thankful they were. She kept to herself that the reason she could watch certain films five and six times was that she didn't care much about story. What she treasured, because they comforted her, were the domestic details, the rooms, the furniture, the clothes, especially the women's clothes and especially their footwear: pumps, heels, saddle shoes, moccasins, cowgirl boots, rain boots, slippers. Only actresses playing peasants or beachgoers ever wore flat-heeled sandals like hers.

She slipped them back on. Harriet, in Rose's first episode, had worn heels. Open-toed, quite high.

℗

She returned calls and drafted next week's newspaper ads. Every so often she looked out the window to monitor the clouds, or she stared at a photograph plate to test her distance vision.

She Googled *car interiors*. She couldn't find David's. She Googled *Harriet Smith*. Up came Harriet Smith radiologists, anesthesiologists, actresses, wedding planners. A narrower search—*Harriet Smith Goldfinch*—brought her to Harriet Smith as an attendee at a literary conference and as an editor mentioned in articles about writers Rose had never heard of. There were no photographs, and *Harriet Smith Toronto* brought nothing.

She went to MySpace. Harriet Smiths aplenty, just all the wrong ones. She tried various people-search sites, pointlessly, since you had to provide a phone number to get an address, or an address to get a phone number. Entering *Harriet Smith* sent her back to the Harriet Smiths she'd already scrolled through on Google.

The phone book offered more hope. It didn't have a listing for Harriet Smith, but there were twenty-five H. Smiths, plus a further six where *H* was the first of two initials, and then nine where an initial preceded the *H*. Forty possibilities. She called H. Smith on Aberdeen Avenue. Nobody would be home in the middle of the day, she told herself.

H. Smith on Aberdeen Avenue was Hailey Smith. Rose phoned the next listing and went into Hugh's voice mail. She kept going. If Harriet answered, she couldn't imagine saying anything other than "Sorry, wrong number." But at least she would have an address to drive past. To park outside of.

A third of the way through the H. Smiths she was surprised by a live person answering, a man. "I won the free tickets," he said.

"Pardon?" said Rose, then realized his caller ID displayed *Regal Theater*.

"The raffle," the man said. "I won, right?"

"No," Rose said. "No, sorry." The raffle was months ago.

"Drat," the man said.

"Actually, I'm looking for someone named Harriet Smith."

"Harriet Smith. The last name rings a bell."

"Sorry to bother you."

"Wait. What's showing tonight?"

"*Once Upon a Time in the West.*"

"What else?"

"It's too long for a second feature."

"I'll bet you sell a lot of drinks during spaghetti Westerns."

"Not"—she began scrolling her cell for messages—"particularly."

"Turn down the air conditioning."

"Okay."

"That's a nice laugh you have."

Had she laughed? "I've got to go."

"You've got to find Harriet."

She switched to her cell, which showed up as *Private Number*, but as if some connecting force had been awakened, she reached a spate of live people. The older the voice, the more help was offered, along the lines of "My cousin Tom might know a Harriet, except we've been out of touch since he made the move to Fort Lauderdale."

She phoned the last dozen numbers with her eye on the advancing storm. She hung up on Y. H. Smith's machine and stood to look out the window.

Minutes passed. Black clouds were approaching, and the servers at the café were lowering the umbrellas. Rose returned to her desk. But the storm held off. When Victor phoned, blue filled the western sky.

"Anything happen?" he asked.

"Nothing," she said. "It missed us here."

"I'm seeing pop-ups on the radar. You might get one in another hour."

Rose's heart skipped. "When?"

"Another hour. Then that should be it until tomorrow."

"Right," she said.

"Oh, and stay away from Wang's."

Mr. Wang, the grandfather, the dumpling maker, worked in the front window. "Sit anywhere," he said as Rose entered.

She paused to ask if they used MSG.

"You not allergic," he told her.

"I don't think I am, but—"

"We no use."

By the time she returned to the theater, more leaden clouds had amassed, and Lloyd stood out front, smoking and surveying the scene. "What's with this weather?" he greeted her.

"You're early."

"My buses dovetailed. Then I go and forget my key." He licked his finger and tapped the spittle on the end of his cigarette.

"Can I bum one of those?" she asked

They crossed the lobby to the kitchen, where he got out his tobacco and rolling papers. They smoked in the alley.

"My first," she coughed.

"This is strong stuff to start with. Homegrown."

"Bring it on."

He pocketed the lighter. "Bad day?"

"Weird day."

"I hear you."

Did he? What constituted weird in his life? Oh, Rose knew—your seventy-four-year-old boss confiding that she sleeps naked. "Just for the record," she said, "my mother sleeps in a full-length nightgown."

"She's feeling frisky," Lloyd said. "More power to her."

"Frisky," Rose said. She looked at a cobweb of cracks in the pavement. Provided her vision didn't suddenly sharpen, and the storm held off, she could stay put. "This is totally foul." She coughed again and leaned against the wall. Inside Harriet's body, cigarette smoke was a soothing vapor.

"Hold on," said Lloyd. He went in and returned with two kitchen chairs.

On the crumbling pavement she had to anchor hers by opening her legs. Positioned thusly, in her long dress, smoking a cigarette that tasted of manure and had been rolled by an aging former convict who wore beat-up cowboy boots, she felt like a pioneer lady, the gritty, strapping one from the movie *Westward the Women.* "She isn't driving you crazy?" she said.

"Not at all," he said.

"She's chewing your ear off, though."

"She's got her stories to tell."

"They aren't all based on fact."

"Is it a fact you were born on the table in there?" He gestured behind himself.

Now, this was interesting. Either her mother had de-liberately avoided mentioning Ava or she had mixed her babies up.

"And your father"—Lloyd chuckled—"he ran into the auditorium and got to deliver the line, 'Is there a doctor in the house?'"

"It was my sister, not me."

"I didn't know you had a sister."

"Ava. She died."

"I'm sorry to hear that."

"Twenty-three years ago. In an accident."

"Shit."

"Pretty much." She pulled longer drags into her raw throat. She expected that soon enough, and without asking, he would get more details from her mother. Or—actually, this was more likely—he would get a complete fabrication designed by Fiona's broken brain to console itself.

A blast of thunder and a sudden downpour had them bringing in the chairs. Rose sprinted to her office, locked the door, and settled behind her desk. There was the spell of anticipation as her vision sharpened and the flecks materialized, then relief as her skin cooled and tightened.

☯

She stood at the doorway of a bathroom. Ivory-tiled walls, white towels, pedestal sink, polished chrome taps, each immaculate feature reassuring to Harriet. She ran her tongue over the narrow vault of her mouth and rubbed one cold bare foot on top of the other. Thunder sounded miles off.

She switched off the light and went down a high-ceilinged hallway to a pale blue bedroom. You could smell the fresh paint. A gust of rain like thrown gravel hit a window in which the bulb from a bedside lamp was reflected. At the edges of her vision were bookshelves and cardboard boxes. A calico cat slept on the bed next to an open manuscript, and she closed the manuscript, put it on the floor, and lay alongside the cat. Her cell beeped. She checked the display: *Incoming Call.*

"Hello?" she answered.

"Did you get the pills?" said a woman.

"Not yet. I'm picking them up later."

"You have to take them with food, or they upset your stomach. You won't feel anything for about a week, but gradually you'll start feeling, you know, just lighter, easier. You'll think, oh, yeah, this is how I'm supposed to feel."

"So how's the physio going?"

"Fine," the woman said impatiently. "But you've got to take them, Harriet. You can't miss a day with antidepressants."

"I know." The conversation was making her anxious. She plucked a cigarette from a pack of Du Mauriers.

"And you've got to stop researching nooses."

She went still. "You were on my computer?"

"I was checking my e-mail."

"You were checking my search history."

"Well, I'm worried about you."

"Did you even feed the cats? They were both yowling when I got home."

"Of course I fed them. Jesus. You tell me you're depressed, I want to help. And then I find out you're researching goddamn nooses."

She fumbled for her lighter. "It calms me down."

"Calms you down."

"I need to know the option of suicide exists, I don't need to act on it. Remember how Dad used to put a cigarette in his mouth but not light it?"

"That was Mom."

"Was it?" She lit her own cigarette. "I thought it was Dad."

"It was Mom."

Along the middle shelves, in front of the books, were statuettes of horses: wooden, ceramic, soapstone, bronze, about two dozen, placed equidistantly. Her gaze paused at a rearing wooden horse, and she got off the bed and went over to it.

"Have you told David?" the sister asked.

She rotated the horse so that it faced forward. "No."

"Are you going to?"

"There's no point if I have an abortion."

"So you've decided."

"Not a hundred percent."

"What kind of man . . ."

Harriet's equilibrium teetered. "Don't start."

"No, I have to say it. What kind of man fools around on his pregnant wife?"

"What kind of woman fools around with a man"— she waved her cigarette—"who *has* a pregnant wife?"

"Well, that's another story. He's going to have to choose."

This provoked a high, jittery laugh. "Between who? Lesley and me, or the babies?"

"Have the baby, then. To hell with him. She doesn't need to know."

"He works down the hall from me."

"I mean she doesn't need to know it's his."

"People find these things out. Anyway, I don't . . . I don't . . ." Her breath caught.

"Okay, honey, it's okay."

☰

The eyes Rose opened were her own. Blood was dripping onto her keyboard, and she yanked out a Kleenex and blew her nose. Compared to the hand that had held the cigarette, this hand felt swollen and clumsy. The rain had let up, and she went to the window. She cried helplessly. Yesterday she'd told herself that the odds of having another episode were astronomical. But it had happened. She stood there, dumbfounded, watching the clouds.

When Victor called she was Googling *antidepressants pregnancy*.

"Well?" he said.

She said yes to the storm, no to the migraine symptoms. Both honest answers, since she'd stopped believing that "silent migraine" described her episodes. She still believed they must be some form of rarefied dream, but she didn't want to get into an argument.

"It was the MSG," Victor said.

Most antidepressants, especially the selective serotonin reuptakes, are generally safe, Rose read. She clicked off the site.

"MSG stimulates a nerve that causes the release of neurotransmitters," Victor went on. "Which causes inflammation of the blood vessels around the brain."

"It's clearing here," she said to change the subject.

"Clear skies overnight. More pop-ups early tomorrow afternoon. Basically, we can expect a similar pattern through to the middle of next week. There's a humid air mass stalled over the whole southern part of the province."

"Thunderstorms every day for a week?" she said, keeping her voice level.

"That's about the size of it."

MAY 1982

The coffin was a Tupperware container. At the sight of the kittens curled up, side by side, Ava snapped out of her stupor and began tucking pieces of Kleenex around the bodies. "They're hibernating," she said.

"A long summer's nap," Fiona said. She went to the barn for a shovel.

Somebody had to do the crying, and it was Rose, although not until later, when she and Ava were in bed.

"Think how safe and warm they are," Ava urged through the heating grates between their rooms.

"I can't."

"Pretend."

Rose made an effort.

"You pretended about Gordon's brains," Ava said. "Oh," she said, "we were so mean to him, and he was so good."

"Carrying you to the house and everything," Rose said. But the sight of Gordon's hand swiping dirt from Ava's legs a little too high up and lingeringly was snarled in Rose's mind with an uncovered skull, and the idea of him disturbed her more than ever.

They followed his advice and every night after supper put out a bowl of Cat Chow. If Duchess ate it, she never showed herself. There were other feral cats slinking around and running off, keeping their distance. The girls began to search, calling her name. Rose shook a bag of Pounce, Ava waved a catnip cigar. Their route took them into their own hayfield, down the first, stunted row of the neighbor's corn, around to the meadow behind the barn, and then into the barn itself, where evidence of Gordon's having collected or deposited his roofing supplies was of absorbing interest to Ava. "He saved Duchess's life," she said reverently, as if he'd leapt in front of a hail of bullets. She refused to entertain their old Gordon fantasies, and dropped her Popsicle-stick knife down the well.

For Rose, the searches gave a spark of meaning to the long, dull days. Their realtor had said that five young girls lived close by, in the farmhouse two concessions over, but he was behind the times. In the farmhouse two concessions over—and it was hardly close by, more like a ten-minute walk—lived an old couple whose grown daughters had left the farm decades ago and who told Fiona they were grateful it wasn't jiggers who had bought Windy Acres.

"Jiggers?" Fiona said.

"What's the new name?" the wife said fretfully, appealing to Ava and Rose.

"Ragheads," her husband muttered from his wooden chair.

"Oh, Sikhs," Fiona said with an uncomfortable laugh. "You mean Sikhs."

"I mean ragheads," he said.

When Rose and Ava weren't searching, they flew the box kite and ran under the sprinkler and walked up the road to visit a herd of cows and feed them dandelion greens through the chain-link fence. They looked for four-leaf clovers in the frame of grass their father kept mowed around the house. Friday mornings they accompanied him into town to do the shopping. He bought household supplies from the BiWay, and Bacardi rum from the Liquor Control Board. Monday mornings the whole family drove to Bert's grocery north of Orangeville. The cigarette-smoking checkout woman, whose neck had the fine wrinkles of a breeze across a pond and whose stomach took the punch of the cash register drawer, raved about Ava's hair, saying every time that it would cost a fortune to get that color at the beauty parlor.

On rainy days Rose might start a jigsaw puzzle. Jigsaw puzzles oppressed Ava. They were vandalized pictures as far as she was concerned, and she worked on them in aggravated spurts. She would rather comb her dolls' hair. Rose's dolls had yet to make it out of the packing box. If she got bored with a puzzle, she helped scrape wallpaper, or she unlocked her diary and wrote down the days' events accompanied by illustrations of cows and pigs and horses copied from her encyclopedia of world mammals. She developed an interest in her mother's books. She read *To Kill a Mockingbird*, and Boo Radley was Gordon until Boo behaved heroically. She read *The Diary of Anne Frank*, and Gordon was the obnoxious Albert Dussel.

They didn't have cable, and the tower picked up only two fuzzy TV channels, so after dinner Rose and Ava watched the PG-rated movies that were sent to their father for consideration in second run. *Amy*, *Neighbors*, *Time Bandits*, *On Golden Pond*. They got in their parents' bed, and Fiona told them Irish ghost stories, which the girls knew word for word but were still frightened by, especially up here at the farm, where the night seemed to go on forever and the wind sounded like banshees.

☾

Every five or six days the wind died, and from miles off, you could hear the barking of dogs and the beeping of gravel trucks. On one such afternoon Ava halted at the entrance to the meadow and said, "I'm tired of doing this."

Rose woke from her searching-for-Duchess trance. "Doing what?"

"Calling and calling."

"She probably found a nice new home," Rose said.

"I don't think she knew her name," Ava said.

The next morning their father told them they'd given it the old college try. He slapped his hands on the kitchen table and said, "How about we adopt a shelter cat? A tame one."

"How about we adopt a goat?" asked Ava prayerfully.

"A goat," he mused.

"I'm not ready to take on farm animals!" Fiona called from the pantry.

"Like in *Heidi*," Ava whispered.

A few mornings later their father said he had to meet a man about a dog and returned not long afterward

79

hauling a rusty trailer. Rose and Fiona were doing the dishes and saw him from the kitchen window.

"Sweet Jesus, what has he gone and done," said Fiona.

"Is it a goat?" asked Ava, who got to him first.

"Better than a goat," their father said. The coils of his hair sprang around. Something green and oily smudged his shirtsleeve. "Seventy bucks including saddle and lessons!" he yelled to Fiona, who stood frowning on the stoop. He unlatched the doors, hooked them to the side, and lowered the ramp. "Come on, boy," he said, tugging the reins.

"A pony!" Ava cried.

"Purebred Shetland," their father said. "His name's Major Tom, but we can change it if you like."

"No, I like Major Tom," Ava said.

"Go ahead and pet him, honey."

Ava stroked a furrow between his ribs. He was cement gray and had a potbelly and a flowing silver mane like a glamour wig.

"How old is he?" Fiona called.

"Twelve."

"He's older than that!"

"He's had a rough life."

"He isn't fixed."

"Sure he is. He's a carnival pony."

They were talking about his penis, the first one, human or animal, Rose had ever seen. It reached his knees. It looked artificial, not a part of his body but something useful, like a lever or crank.

"Here's Gordon with the saddle," their father said.

"Gordon?" Ava said. His truck pulled into the driveway, and she dashed toward it, her arm-flailing run. Then, as if embarrassed by her enthusiasm, she ran back to her mother.

"Mornin', ladies," said Gordon, climbing out.

"How's your cut, Gordon?" Ava asked shyly, her fists pushed under her chin.

"Healed up good, Red." He extended his chubby arm. "Thanks to your mother."

Fiona shrugged. "Thanks to antiseptic cream." But she smiled and wiped her hands on her apron.

Their father was poking in the rear of the truck. "Which is Major Tom's?"

"I got it, Mr. Bowan," said Gordon. He strode around and hoisted out a worn saddle, a dirty Hudson's Bay blanket, and a cardboard box. "Okay, girls, if you care to watch."

Ava skipped to his side.

"We start with the blanket," said Gordon, and threw it over Major Tom's back. "Like so." He tugged at it, smoothing it out. "Next comes the saddle." He set the saddle on the blanket. "Like so." He slapped Major Tom's rump, cruelly hard, it seemed to Rose. "Now for the girth. The girth goes under."

Rose looked at the cornfield. All you had to do not to get lost in a cornfield was stick to your row. To find your way out of a maze, you ran your hand against one wall and never lifted it. If a current dragged you out to sea, you swam parallel to the shore. These and other survival techniques Rose had read in a book called *Stayin' Alive*.

"Rose," said her father, his loud voice penetrating her fog. "Would you like the first ride?"

"That's okay," said Rose. She worried that her weight would be too much for the pony. "Ava can go."

Gordon guessed what she was balking at. "He's stronger'n he looks."

"I don't believe in riding on animals' backs," Rose said, humiliated. She went into the house and sat at the kitchen table. A few minutes later her father summoned her back out for instructions on cleaning the stall and feeding and currying Major Tom.

This she took to. Major Tom was the most docile animal. You could comb his mane, and he might graze you with his red-rimmed eyes, but his mind seemed placidly elsewhere. When you brushed his rump, urine dripped from his penis, but that was just Major Tom. Good old Major Tom. Rose declared herself the official groom, and her father stopped bothering her to ride and had her and Ava outfitted at Saddle-Up Equestrian. Rose got green rubber boots, green rubber gloves, and blue coveralls. Ava got black boots, white jodhpurs, a red helmet, and a navy jacket.

When Ava appeared all decked out for her lessons, proud and self-conscious, Rose felt protective, although Gordon touched her only to help her mount and dismount, holding her by the waist, and this seemed harmless enough. What passed between Rose and Gordon was "How's it going, Rosie?" and "Fine," until one morning he strolled over to where she sat on the split-rail fence and said, "You look out for your little sister, eh, Rosie?"

"There's nothing else to do," she murmured.

"No, it's good. My stepdaughters, they fight like a pair of weasels." His eyes followed Ava, who was trotting Major Tom around an orange construction cone. "Last month the older one knocked out the younger one's front tooth with a pool cue."

Rose looked at him. "On purpose?"

"Hard to tell with them two." He squinted at the sky. "They're about your age. What are you?" He gave her a glance. "Thirteen?"

"Eleven," Rose said and jumped off the fence.

He started back to Ava. "I'll bring 'em around one day," he called over his shoulder.

THURSDAY, JUNE 30, 2005

Rose tried to get back to writing her ad copy, but the exchange between Harriet and her sister kept running through her mind. *What kind of man fools around on his pregnant wife? What kind of woman fools around with a man who* has *a pregnant wife?* In her hand and arm she seemed to feel the sensation of Harriet waving the cigarette around, just as her father used to wave around his cigar when he talked on the phone.

And then she was thinking about her father and his lung cancer. Stage four by the time it was diagnosed, and so rampant or so discouraging to him that in a matter of days he went from singing arias at the top of his lungs to wheezing tunelessly, from hugging the breath out of people to patting their shoulders. The morphine gave him delusions. She'd forgotten this, but she remembered it now, him hallucinating about squatters in the lobby ("There's plenty of space," he reasoned) and catastrophe in his general affairs. One morning he shuffled by her desk and said, "We're broke, honey, I'm sorry," and she panicked before escaping the office and phoning their bank.

She'd been only a year out of university, still learning the ropes, and there she was doing ninety percent of the work while he lay on the sofa and touched his head with the faltering swipes of a man who can't figure out where his hair has gone. Sometimes he leafed through photo albums and broke into little bullfrog moans, at pictures of Ava, she imagined, after which he holed up in the projection booth and listened to his Édith Piaf records. Before dinner he opened an office window and smoked. Why had Rose never joined him? She needn't have started with cigars, she could have smoked cigarettes. She wondered why she'd never at least given it a try.

She tapped her mouth. Was it possible to develop a craving so quickly? Apparently so. She grabbed her purse and went down to the lobby.

Fiona was filing her nails under the white light of the menu board. "Where are you off to?" she asked when Rose opened the register.

"I thought I'd get dinner," Rose said. She helped herself to a ten-dollar bill (what did cigarettes cost?) and then to another ten.

"Get enough for Lloyd," Fiona said. "He's joining us. He'll be joining us from now on, if you have no objections."

He was coming around the corner as Rose left the theater. She motioned him away from the windows and asked for a cigarette. "I'm buying my own," she said. "I just need one to tide me over."

"I'm not sure I should be encouraging this," he said, but he put down her father's wooden toolbox, near the wall where the pavement was dry, and took a rolled cigarette out of one of the compartments. "Did Fiona tell you about the dinner thing?" he asked, digging in the front pocket of his pants for the lighter.

"Yeah, it makes sense," Rose said. "If you're okay with it."

"Me? Sure, I'm okay. Free meal, good company." He lit the cigarette and handed it to her.

"Don't tell my mother about this," she said.

"You're the boss."

"Don't tell her that, either."

She set off, puffing and hacking. She deliberately smoked the way Harriet did—quick inhalations, a sideways tug of her head on the exhale.

She resolved to lose ten pounds. She'd been dieting half her life, but over the past few years she'd given up because Victor liked large women. Now it felt slovenly, all the food she ate, all the space she occupied compared to Harriet, who would get bigger as the months passed if she kept the baby. *Keep it*, Rose thought, a sudden, instinctive appeal. In effect, and the absurdity was not lost on her, she lobbied her own unconscious.

When she got back to the theater, Fiona was reading the newspaper at the kitchen table. "There's iced tea," she said.

Rose poured herself a glass. Her throat felt parched.

"Nobody dies anymore," Fiona said. "They leave. They pass away. They pass. 'After a courageous battle with cancer, Donald passed.' Passed what? Wind? Do you know what I want mine to say?"

"What?" Rose asked reluctantly.

"Bowan, Fiona. Dead." She reached between the salt and pepper shakers for her playing cards. "How about some honeymoon bridge?"

Rose glanced at the clock.

"There's time," Fiona said.

She was an expert shuffler. She had learned from her aunt Aileen, who as a young woman in Limerick dealt the poker games played above a milliner's shop. Despite years of practice Rose had never progressed beyond a common dovetail shuffle. Fiona could do the Hindu, which is when you slide packets of cards from the top of the deck and let them fall into your other hand. "Cut," she said and smacked the deck down.

The score soon mounted in her favor. "You're letting me win," she said.

"I'm not," Rose said. But neither was she paying much attention. She was barely keeping her eyes open.

"One day you'll be letting me win," Fiona said. "And then the day will come when I won't know a pack of cards from a pack of wolves. On that day"—she trumped Rose's ace with a three—"you can do with your old mother what you want."

A silence opened between them. Rose wasn't sure if she'd just been given permission to move her mother into a nursing home when the time came. "We'll do what *you* want," she said emotionally, thinking of Victor's mother.

Fiona laughed. "Don't leave it up to me."

Dinner was burritos, chips, and salsa. Afterward Rose went out to the alley and smoked a cigarette with the homeless men—the brothers, everybody called them, two unrelated guys of indeterminate age, not young. Around noon they started collecting cans and bottles in a lopsided, three-wheeled wagon until they had enough to buy a jug of red wine. They did their drinking in any of four or five back doorways, and because they were quiet and picked up their garbage, even their cigarette butts, the local businesses let them be. Sometimes Fiona brought them popcorn, which they accepted politely. They were more enthusiastic about the cigarettes Rose offered this evening. The tall one exhaled his first drag skyward and said to Rose, without looking at her, "Your heartbeat is fast."

"It is?" she said. "How can you tell?"

He pointed under her ear.

She touched the place and felt the throbbing.

"He knows what he's talking about," the short one said. "He's Iroquois Indian."

The tall one squinted with something like professional skepticism. "Have you been on a plane recently?" he asked.

"No," she said.

"Jet lag speeds up the heart."

It might have been the power of suggestion, but when she was back inside, her tiredness had a jet-lag buzz. She helped at the snack bar, and then she climbed to her office, so exhausted from the stairs that she couldn't muster the energy to clear a space for herself on the sofa, and curled up on the carpet instead.

"Hey, hey, hey, hey, hey," she heard through the floor. "If you want any tickets, you'll have to go around to, eh, to, eh, the front of the, eh, oooh, well."

That was probably the longest line of dialogue in the entire movie. The screenplay for *Once Upon a Time in the West* was 265 pages, but as her father had calculated, the dialogue alone amounted to a mere 15 pages. Rose decided she should post this tidbit on the Regal's website.

Her cell rang. She let it go into messaging. After five minutes she reached for it and pressed *play*.

"Hi, it's me," said Victor's voice. "There's a pop-up on the radar."

Rose stood and went to the window. Blue sky in all directions.

"ETA half an hour. And, oh, yeah. I was able to get a background check on Lloyd."

What was this?

"He served his sentence at Joyceville. In 1988 he participated in a recreation-yard brawl. One inmate stabbed, life-threatening injuries. Attacker, or attackers, unidentified—"

She hung up. Who appointed him to be Lloyd's parole officer? A guy gets stabbed in a brawl almost twenty years ago, big deal. How did Victor even know that

91

Lloyd hadn't tried to pull the fighters apart? Well, he'd better not say anything to her mother. Or to Lloyd.

She lit a cigarette and tried to maintain her indignation, but it soon got muscled aside by the memory of Harriet's bedroom. She tapped ash out the window. Dark clouds were boiling above the Pepsi billboard. The wind picked up, the marquee cables made their low, zooming whistle. She shut the window, locked the door, sat at her desk, and stared at the plate beneath the photograph of her father and Groucho Marx.

With the first stirring of thunder the words became legible. The flecks arrived, the fortresses assembled, prompting the nausea, prompting a sensation of Harriet's skeleton crystallizing out of the ghost of Rose's own.

℗

She was lying on a mat and looking with Harriet's perfect vision at an acoustic-tile ceiling.

"That's it, that's right," said a man in a deep, sympathetic voice. "Give yourself over to the feeling." He had an English accent. The thunder was a faint rumble, and he said, "There it goes. Sink into it. The calm after the storm."

Harriet was far from calm. All around her people breathed audibly.

The man said, "Roll onto your stomachs," but it hurt her breasts to lie on her stomach, and ahead of his directions she crouched and began to straighten. Her eyes traveled up her boyish body: gray track pants, a pink tank top. In the wall behind her, water gurgled down a drain.

It was then, during her fourth episode, hearing the water, that Rose grew aware of herself, not as a glint at the edge of Harriet's consciousness but as a separate consciousness, a fully integrated component. She wasn't surprised. She felt as if she had been waiting for this from the start.

What surprised her was the instructor. Rather than the slim and elegant person she had imagined from his accent, he was a bull-shouldered, florid-faced guy with a bushy moustache and crooked, red-framed glasses duct-taped at the hinges. A former football player gone slightly to seed was her impression. And yet his smile imparted alertness and alacrity. He bowed his head and offered a yogic blessing, and the students returned it in ragged union. When his eyes rested on her, Harriet melted a little. She loved him, but not sexually. There was no excitement in the feeling.

People began rolling up their mats. "My basement's a lake," said her neighbor to someone else.

"You came," murmured a voice behind her.

Silent, in bare feet, the instructor had appeared. "Oh, Marsh." She squeezed his arm. "I had no idea you could stand on your head."

"Optical illusion."

She smiled.

"Old ashram trick." He adjusted his glasses in a precise and delicate way at odds with the glasses themselves and with the entire look of him. "One second," he said and laid a fleshy hand on her shoulder while he exchanged a few words with another student. "Sorry I didn't introduce you," he said when the student was out of earshot. "I can never remember his bloody name."

They started across the room. From overhead came a burst of loud music, quickly turned down. "Is that the party starting?" she asked.

"You're staying, I hope." He flipped off a bank of lights. "Sandra's bringing a karaoke machine."

"Oh, God."

"We could perform a duet together, you and I."

"No, we couldn't."

A few students were waiting for him in the corridor. She hung back and put on her shoes. When he rejoined her, she said, "Why aren't you even a tiny bit angry with me, a tiny bit sulky?"

He slipped into a pair of worn rubber sandals. "Do you think you're the first person ever to have stood me up?"

"Yes."

"You're one amongst a teeming multitude."

They smiled at each other. He's in love with her, Rose thought. It was plain enough that she couldn't understand how Harriet held his gaze.

"Stay," he said.

"I can't. I'm sorry."

"Harriet, Harriet, Harriet." He wrapped his thick arms around her and rocked her from side to side. With the mat and her elbows between their bodies, it was awkward but nice. "We have a buffet. You remember buffets? Hard-boiled eggs and jellied salads."

"I've got a four-hundred-page manuscript to plow through."

"Don't plow. Skim. Glide."

She had to laugh. "I need to go home first, but maybe I can come back later."

His arms opened. "See how easy that was."

"I'm not promising anything."

"And yet my hopes are up."

She started walking off. "Bye, Marsh."

"If you play your cards right, I might even ask you to dance."

She entered the women's changing room. At the lockers she unfastened a key pinned to the inside of her waistband and opened locker number eight. She pulled off her tights and T-shirt and removed a flimsy red dress from a pink padded hanger. Harriet's mood took a sexual swerve. Rose strained to hear her thoughts, to break down the wall. Her own thought, her exhilarated certainty, was that Harriet was meeting David.

☽

One second Rose was inside Harriet, putting on the red dress, the next she was back in her own body. She clutched the solid flesh of her legs and arms. Her eyes streamed tears. Why this sadness? she wondered. Harriet hadn't been sad.

She turned on the lamp. The Toronto directory was still under her phone, and she flipped through the pages to the *Y*s. Yoga, Yoga Studios.

Mostly she reached voice mail. On something like her tenth try, yet another recorded message came on, and she was about to hang up when a live woman said, "Fruit of Life."

Rose asked for Marsh. By now she was convinced there was no such person.

"Marsh!" called the woman.

"Wait—"

"Good evening."

That deep, English-accented voice. At the sound of it Rose didn't faint or die. On the contrary, she crashed to life. Short, tough gasps pumped from her belly.

"Is that you, Kimberly?" he said.

"No," she said. "It's Violet." Violet was her second name. He asked what he could do for her, and she touched the ellipsis her lamp had spawned on the chrome paperweight and said, "A friend of mine took one of your classes, and, um, she told me about it."

"Okay."

"So . . ." This was impossible, excruciating. "So I was phoning to see if you, if you teach a Saturday class."

"I do. I teach a beginning-level hatha at ten and an intermediate at two thirty."

"Two thirty," she said.

"For your first time we ask that you arrive early. Two fifteen."

"Two fifteen."

"What are you doing right now, Violet?"

What was Rose doing? She was robotically repeating the ends of his sentences.

"We're having a party, here at the center," he said. "It's just getting under way. You're welcome—"

Rose threw down the phone.

Silent explosions discharged in her head. It was barely conceivable that on her own, before Harriet, she had heard about the yoga center and Marsh and had brought this knowledge to the episodes. But how did she know about the party? How could she have brought *that* to an episode?

"Please hang up and try your call again."

"What?" she said, terrified.

"Please hang up. This is a recording."

"Okay, it's okay," she said. She retrieved the phone and jabbed *end*. She wasn't losing her mind. Knowing more than you could possibly know wasn't insanity, it was telepathy.

On the windowsill a wet pigeon dipped its head and examined her with an orange eye. The episodes were not some exotic form of dream life, they were actually happening. Every time she thought she was entering Harriet, she really was. She looked closely at her hands and arms. Surely her body didn't travel as well, at such speed, returning intact. The sense of her flesh shrinking, surely she only imagined it.

She got out her mirror again, took off her glasses, and examined her face closely for signs of change, of damage. The harder she looked the more she longed to see Harriet's face, to confirm her existence, as she'd just confirmed Marsh's.

She told Fiona and Lloyd that she was going to meet her friend Robin for a drink. Robin and her husband were having problems, she said. She promised to be back before the end of the movie.

She took the car. Pink sky glazed the puddles. She wondered at her ability to distinguish Harriet's emotions from her own and figured it must be like distinguishing fact from conjecture, or present circumstances from memory. She had the pulled-thread sensation beneath her skin.

The yoga center was in a converted factory on Carlaw Avenue. A professionally painted sign said, FRUIT OF LIFE YOGA CENTER—CLASSES, THAI MASSAGE, TEACHER TRAINING, AND STUDIOS. A handwritten sign said, *Party Upstairs.*

Rose went downstairs.

That the hallway was the one from her last episode made her head swim. She reached the changing room and pushed the door's metal plate.

The sinks seemed lower, and it took her a moment to understand that this was because she was a good six inches taller than Harriet. She dug in her purse, found a quarter, and opened locker number eight. The pink padded hanger was there, the hanger that Harriet had touched. She pressed it to her pounding heart, then shoved it as far as it would go into her purse and hung the purse on the hook. The key she put in her pocket.

Above the brawl of voices they were playing panpipe music. It drew her hypnotically up the stairs, along another hallway, into a packed room.

She located Marsh among a crowd of young men to the guffawing amusement of whom he was demonstrating robotic dance moves. There he was. Not a dream, not a vision. He had changed into a shiny red shirt, blue jeans, and a belt with a silver buckle the size of a hamburger patty. A cowboy-disco look, except he still wore his rubber sandals.

She searched for Harriet. A young woman with a buzz cut smiled at her invitingly, and although Rose kept searching, the woman inched over and snaked an arm around her waist. "Don't be sad," she pouted.

"I'm not sad," Rose said.

"What's your name?"

"Violet."

"No," the woman said, "way." She withdrew her arm. "I'm Violet."

"We've got a regular flower show going on," quipped a guy to Rose's left.

"Would you happen to know someone named

Harriet Smith?" Rose asked.

Violet shook her head.

"I know a *lock*smith," said the funny guy.

"Thanks anyway," Rose said and burrowed into the room, glad of her height. The music was now "Back in the U.S.S.R." People were dancing. A vision came to her of Harriet and David necking, and she was wounded, not by jealousy but by the far more absurd feeling of abandonment: the two of them going ahead without her. She lost Marsh, then found him again at the buffet table. He was with a woman pushing a walker. The room seemed to tilt in their direction.

"My stuffed mushrooms," the woman was saying.

"Is that goat cheese?" Marsh asked.

"Herb-and-garlic. Try one."

"I intend to try many."

"Well, don't wait forever. They go fast." The woman moved her walker farther along. "My spring rolls."

"Let's put those near the front," said Marsh. He reached for the plate, and Rose slipped in behind him.

"My salsa pockets," said the woman.

"They look delicious," Rose found the wherewithal to say.

"Try one," said the woman. She scooped up the biggest, set it on a napkin, and passed it to Marsh, who went to pass it to Rose. But at his touch they both got a shock so powerful he dropped it.

"Bugger," he said. It had landed on his sandal. "Sorry, Helen."

"Nonsense," said the woman.

"It's my fault," said Rose. She had a giddy, euphoric feeling. "I gave you a shock."

"You gave each other a shock," said Helen. "I heard it." She shoved napkins at Marsh. "All that lightning must be electrifying the air."

From his crouch Marsh smiled at Rose. "Are you burnt to a cinder?"

She laughed. "I don't think so."

People were squeezing by, and once he was standing, he put his hand on her shoulder to encourage her to step aside. No shock this time, only that penetrating warmth she remembered from when he put his hand on Harriet's shoulder. "Where's the recycling?" he asked, looking around.

"Here," said Helen. She snatched the napkins and poked them into a plastic bag that hung from the walker's crossbar. To Rose she said, "Take another one. They go fast." She thumped her walker in a semicircle. "I need to use the facilities," she announced. Off she went onto the dance floor, straight through dancing couples.

"Proof that angels live among us," Marsh said, and Rose, who'd been on the verge of laughing again, altered her expression. "Now you," Marsh said, clasping his hands. "You need a plate."

"That's okay," Rose said. "I'm not really hungry."

"Something to drink? We have twenty varieties of juice. Apple, banana-grape, blueberry." He was listing them on his fingers. "I'm Marsh, by the way."

"Rose," she said, to disassociate herself from the dimwit he'd spoken to on the phone.

"Cranberry, cranberry-raspberry. I have to go alphabetically."

I saw you in my mind, Rose rehearsed. An hour ago. You were teaching a yoga class. You had on a white T-shirt and navy track pants. His smile would waver but courteously hold. As evidence she would recite phrases from his and Harriet's conversation. He would assume she had eavesdropped. "I'm good, thanks," she said.

He studied her. He stroked his jaw. He had a repertoire of convivial poses. "I'm trying to remember where I've seen you. It wasn't in a class."

He might have spotted her at the Regal, but she preferred to think she carried a trace of Harriet. Suppressed laughter convulsed her chest. Why was it all so hilarious? She turned her attention to the dancers and craned to see Harriet among them. For yoga types drinking fruit juice, they were a rambunctious bunch.

"You've lost somebody," he said.

"I'm looking for somebody."

"Perhaps I can help you."

"Harriet Smith."

"Harriet," he said, adjusting his glasses. "She isn't here. She couldn't make it."

"Oh," she said, sobered.

"Are you a friend of hers?"

"A friend of a friend," she said and instantly regretted it. Why would a friend of a friend imagine Harriet might be here, when only an hour ago Harriet had still been making up her mind?

But either the question didn't occur to Marsh, or he chose not to pursue it. He took his glasses off and twisted the tape that held the arm in place. "I should buy one of those miniature repair kits," he said.

He sounded frustrated, lovelorn. Out of the ruins of Rose's own hope, a pain for him moved her to say, "She's missing an awesome party."

He put the glasses on. "She is, isn't she?" he said, brightening.

Rose suspected that David and Harriet were still together. Or maybe David had left, and Harriet was alone and unhappy. Rose's need to see her rebounded with sickening force.

"Would you like to risk mutual combustion?" Marsh said.

"Pardon?" she said.

"Shall we dance?"

"Oh, okay. Sure."

The music was "Ob-La-Di, Ob-La-Da." He steered her through a number of fancy turns, and she took a breath and said, "You wouldn't happen to know Harriet's address, would you?"

He leaned back to see her face. "Why do you ask?"

"I have a manuscript I'm supposed to give her." She winced apologetically. "I know, it's the last thing an editor wants at a party, but I promised I'd try to pass it along."

"I can give it to her." Their dancing had dwindled to swaying back and forth. "I'll be seeing her soon."

Rose freed her hands. "Ob-La-Di, Ob-La-Da" had segued to "Chain of Fools," and women were strutting onto the dance floor. "Thank you," she said, "but I'm driving, so I could just as easily stick it in her mailbox. If she doesn't live in Scarborough or somewhere."

"Not that far away. She moved a few weeks ago."

"Oh, really? Where to?"

"The west end," he said, with a smile for a woman who was finger-snapping her way over.

"This is our song!" the woman cried.

He let himself be tugged by his belt buckle. "I'm sure if you drop it by her office, it'll get to her," he called to Rose.

Right up until he said "the west end," she'd felt trusted. She should have strung the conversation out, talked about neighborhoods and streets, only gradually circling in on a specific area. She looked at her watch. Five after ten. She escaped the party and hurried to the changing room for her purse. She couldn't get the hanger any farther in, so she concealed it by holding the purse under her arm, the hanger's silk padding cool and soft against her bare skin.

There was a sheet of fog some fifteen feet off the ground. It made for such a convincing impression of a low ceiling that everyone drove cautiously. The west end covered a lot of ground, but even so, she was tempted to turn west in the hopes of picking up a psychic charge. Like those people who cruised around searching for free Wi-Fi.

She fingered a cigarette from her pack. She was shivering and sweating, feverish. You're in the middle of a miracle, she thought. This is how a miracle feels.

Who could she tell? Not Victor. Worse than challenging her sanity, he would advance his "You've got a lot on your plate" theory, which, frankly, *attacked* her sanity by implying that, given enough stress, she competed with her mother to see who could manufacture the most elaborate delusion.

Her poor mother. Memory by memory Fiona was losing herself, while she, in the most concrete way possible, was finding another self.

FRIDAY, JULY 1, 2005

She dreamed she was a young girl among bad-tempered people who were her family, although she didn't recognize anybody. "Hit her, someone," squawked the grandmother when Rose wept about being served a fish with the head still on.

She woke up and saw the pink padded hanger on her bedside table. All over again she was awestruck. She felt materially altered, lighter, her extremities colder, her heart rate faster, as if while she'd been sunk in normal sleep her entire cellular structure had reconfigured. She put her glasses on, and the fact of the miracle beamed from her dresser and bookcase. They *knew*, these things. Her Sony clock radio, conduit to voices and frequencies, certainly knew. She dialed around for a top-of-the-hour weather report.

Victor's forecast kept changing. Late last night he'd said the storm would arrive closer to three. This was during their bedtime phone call, in the aftermath of an argument they'd had, and not entirely resolved, about him taking it upon himself to research Lloyd's prison record.

"The Weather Network is saying between one and two," she'd said, still angry apparently, since it pleased her to contradict him.

"They're wrong," he said. "Are you worried about a migraine?"

"Mom does her shopping at three. I'm worried about her driving in a downpour."

"She shouldn't be driving, period."

"She's fine when she's driving, she doesn't have strokes when she's driving," Rose said testily, understanding that this was the case only so far, but she didn't like him ruling on her mother's faculties.

680 News was now calling for the storm to hit sometime after twelve. Where they and Victor were in agreement was with the probability of the humid air mass hanging around until the middle of next week.

And then what? Would the episodes be over, or was the trigger simply a thunderstorm, any thunderstorm from any air mass? In which case Rose would enter Harriet ten, fifteen, twenty times a year until one of them died. Right now the episodes were addictive, but the prospect of them never ending, of her entire life being split between two worlds, was terrifying. Don't think too far ahead, she told herself. One thunderstorm, one day at a time. She went to the window and opened the drapes.

Fiona was out there, kneeling on her cushion, weeding the garden. Rose tapped the pane, only to say good morning, but Fiona stood and walked over, a grim cast to her face.

Rose cranked the window open. "You're up early," she said. Warm, humid air poured in.

"Get the binoculars," Fiona muttered.

"What?"

"He's spying on me."

Rose needed a second to realize. "Mom," she said sinkingly, "he's inside."

"He's been peeking through the living room drapes. Get the binoculars, you'll see." She glanced over her shoulder. In the same moment Charles came out onto the porch, and she cringed back around and said, "Is he looking?"

"No."

"What's he doing?"

"He's going to the sofa. He's sitting down." For the first time since the heat wave he wasn't wearing a suit jacket. He had on a vest, though, and a long-sleeved shirt and a tie. "Now he's getting a cigarette. Okay, now he's looking." She waved.

"Don't wave," Fiona hissed.

Charles raised his hand.

"Did he see you?"

"Yep." In a gust of fellow feeling she added, "He comes out to smoke."

"They have a perfectly nice patio."

"You can weed later."

Fiona's jaw hardened. "I weed in the morning." She strode to the cushion, elbows working.

Rose showered and dressed and fixed herself a crash-diet breakfast of black coffee and muesli with skim milk. To burn off even that, she planned on walking to the theater. She put the hanger in her briefcase.

High cirrus clouds were pushing in when she left the house, and Fiona had progressed to digging moss from between the paving stones, the very moss it had taken her years to grow.

Victor was right, Rose thought. Her mother shouldn't be driving. "Mom," she said, "let's do the grocery shopping together."

Fiona pitched a clump of moss into the bucket. "You know, it's not my business if you're having an affair," she said.

A pulse started up in Rose's throat. "What are you talking about?"

"Is he looking?"

"He's"—Rose squinted—"asleep."

Fiona turned her head cautiously. "He's pretending. He does that."

"Why would you think I'm having an affair?"

"He's watching me under his eyelids."

"When would I have time for an affair?" Rose persisted. "Who would I have one *with*?"

"I just want you to know, I don't blame you," Fiona said primly. "I'm sure Victor is no bargain in the bedroom."

Rose gave up. "I'll be back before three," she said. "You'll wait, right?"

"For what?" Fiona looked at her.

"For me to go shopping with you."

"You want to go shopping?"

"Yes."

"Well." A sigh. "Don't be late then."

As soon as she turned the corner, she lit a cigarette. She couldn't get over her mother's acuity. If kissing David with Harriet's lips didn't qualify as an affair, in terms of pleasure it felt like nothing less. From the shreds of her mother's disintegrating brain, new networks must be forming. Freak networks, telepathic transmitters.

She cut through the park. On this holiday Friday the playground area was crowded, and she didn't notice the little boy toddling toward her until they almost collided.

"Dat!" he yelled and pointed at her stomach. He wore only a diaper.

Rose held her cigarette out of harm's way. "Where's your mommy?"

Extreme expressions vied for his face. "Dat!" he yelled again, stabbing his finger, and a man—the father, presumably—caught him and swung him off the path. The boy wriggled to keep Rose in sight.

Rose walked on. She figured she must remind the boy of an aunt or family friend. Then she wondered if she was emitting a signal that young children—fresh arrivals from the ether—recognized. To get completely irrational about it, she wondered if her stomach hadn't captivated him because he knew about Harriet's threatened abortion and as a recent fetus himself was expressing his alarm.

What can I do? Rose thought. It's her body. All the same, she couldn't help feeling she had a stake in this pregnancy. It might even be argued that during the episodes *she* was pregnant, she and Harriet together, conjoined mothers.

No students were loitering in front of the theater, not today. Rose headed straight for her office and checked Victor's forecast on Environment Canada. Like his counterparts at 680 News and the Weather Network he was calling for the storm to hit around noon. A little over an hour to go, then.

She took out the hanger and squeezed the padding and rubbed it on her face. To anyone else it was just a hanger. To her it was a physical object that had crossed the uncanny chasm between Harriet's life and her own.

Once, watching a dish detergent bubble sail around the kitchen, her father, the avowed atheist, said, "For all we know, that's an angel." Rose also identified as an atheist, and yet from her mother's lapsed Catholic side she petitioned God in moments of spiking want or fear. So did most people, she suspected. People might not say, "Please, *God*," but when they said, "Please," and "Come on," weren't they appealing to a force capable of affecting outcomes?

She put the hanger on the sofa, where she could see it from her desk. She opened the windows and turned on the air conditioner. Normally she was careful about wasting electricity, but a few dollars down the drain was preferable to her mother smelling cigarette smoke. She read comments on the Regal's website and found a debate in progress as to whether or not the residents of the *Rear Window* apartments were exhibitionists.

"Even the murderer doesn't shut his blinds at crucial moments. For example, when he's washing blood off his bathroom walls! What's with that?"

"It's boiling outside. 92F!"

"People were more open in those days. They were only a generation or two removed from the intimacy of life in shtetls and rural villages."

"But the characters aren't open. Their blinds are! Leaving Jimmy Stewart out of it, they're closed off from each other."

"They take for granted that their right to privacy is respected by their neighbors. Stewart violates a tacit code."

Again, Rose felt morally challenged. Okay, she was violating somebody's privacy, but not deliberately, she didn't make the episodes happen. On the other hand, she couldn't wait for them. Being in that streamlined, percolating body with its loose joints and eagle vision was an indescribable thrill, beyond anything she had ever felt or imagined feeling.

A stunning thought came to her. Harriet might have gone into work. She might pick up her phone.

Rose dialed Goldfinch's number. Two rings, three. She reached the directory, typed H-A-R. The message clicked on, and she listened just long enough to hear Harriet's name being said. A split second before the beep, she hung up.

Now she was too restless to work. She needed a cup of chamomile tea, she decided. But once she was downstairs a different impulse struck her, and she switched on the houselights and entered the auditorium. Down the aisle she went, to row H, seat eleven, the best seat in the house according to her father, although whenever he had watched a movie in here he'd sat in the back row of the balcony to be inconspicuous and to survey his empire.

Rose stroked the armrests. She ran her fingers between the brass lion claws that covered the ends. Thousands upon thousands of fingers had felt these grooves. Rose lifted her hands and put them down again more lightly. She became aware of the springs beneath her hips and how lumpy they would feel to hips as fleshless as Harriet's.

She pulled down the seats on either side of her. She studied the red leather, worn as a rock face but not cracked, not yet. She pushed the seats back up, pulled them down again. She was thinking of a game she and Ava used to play, where they flipped down certain seats in certain rows to make giant patterns—triangles and crosses and letters—which they then admired from the balcony. They spoke to each other in sexy French accents in the balcony because the man who designed the wrought-iron railing had been French and had also invented the underwire bra. They treasure-hunted throughout the theater, digging between the cushions for pens, jewelry, money; there were always a few coins. Once they found a silver matchbox containing only a piece of paper that had the word *menstruation* written on it. The girls knew what menstruation was, and they laughed giddily, but then, impressed by the box's navy velvet lining, and also by the formidable, still-perplexing business itself—monthly, unstoppable bleeding—they were solemn. Ava said, "A lady must have dropped it." Rose said, "Or a vampire."

She couldn't remember what they did with that note. The box they would have put in the lost-and-found drawer.

It was 11:45 but already dark outside when she left the auditorium. She hurried up to her office, retrieved the hanger, and held it with both hands like a divining rod. A divining rod whose curved end pointed back at herself. She sat in her chair. The thunder sounded far away, but her vision was crisp and the flecks were appearing. During the nausea, she shut her eyes.

Φ

She was standing in the same bathroom from her third episode. She had on white underpants and an orange T-shirt. The thunder here was closer: long, booming rolls.

Her feet were icy. Her nerves were frayed. She lifted her shirt, angled herself, and pushed her belly out. She wasn't showing, or hardly at all. She pulled the shirt higher. One juvenile breast came into view.

I shouldn't be seeing this, Rose thought. *Look up*, she implored. *Look in the mirror.*

She looked in the mirror. She held her own gaze. Rose tried to catch herself, the slightest, lurking presence.

But just as in the second episode, it was Ava's eyes Rose saw. Not simply eyes reminiscent of Ava's, but the same green with the fold underneath, the same shape and restless frown.

Other resemblances between Ava and Harriet now rushed at Rose: the eagle vision, the cold extremities, the anxiety, the meticulousness, the nail biting. Why hadn't she recognized any of this before? If it was possible to cry inside another person's body, Rose cried.

Harriet was still agitated. She turned from the mirror and went down the hall to her bedroom. The calico cat was sleeping on the bed again, and she lay alongside it and scratched its head. It had fishy breath and fish-shaped eyes ringed with black lines that extended from the corners like tail fins. Its purr was a racket but calming to Harriet. She rolled over and reached for the phone.

"Harriet," answered a thick male voice.

"Oh, no, I woke you."

"I'm awake. Theoretically." It was Marsh.

She slid a cigarette from the pack on the bedside table. "What time did you get in last night?"

"Late. Quarter to three."

"Yikes."

"I'm guessing the manuscript kept you spellbound till the wee hours."

A fluttering in her belly told Rose that there was no manuscript. "I packed it in around midnight," she said. She got her cigarette lit and exhaled away from the cat. "A quarter to three. That's a lot of karaoke."

"Like you, the machine failed to make an appearance. We danced. *I* danced. I was the belle of the ball."

"Of course you were."

"I scarcely missed you." He yawned. "Someone else did, however."

"Who?"

Rose felt as if she held her breath.

"A flower name."

"Daisy?"

There was a roar of thunder. "Is that at your end?" he said.

"You'll be getting it soon," she said.

"Rose," he said.

"I don't know any Roses."

"She had a manuscript for you. She wanted your address."

"You didn't give it to her, I hope."

"Certainly not."

"What did she look like?"

"What did she look like." More yawning. "Tall. Voluptuous. Dark, curly hair. Medusa hair. Soulful eyes."

"Soulful eyes." She smiled and tapped her cigarette above the ashtray. "Everybody you meet has soulful eyes."

"Can you hold for two minutes?"

"Go pee. I just wanted to know how the party went."

"Two minutes."

"It's okay. I'm going to try to work. I'll call you later."

She took the ashtray and lighter and left the bedroom. The cat trotted ahead, tail high. Past the bathroom, past a narrow office (desk, stacks of books and papers), into a kitchen with vacant counters and a round wooden table. Harriet seemed to be thinking hard. Rose was thinking, soulful eyes. She was marveling at the coincidence of being in Harriet at exactly the moment she heard herself described.

A black-and-white cat slept on the window ledge. She put the ashtray down and massaged its haunches. Its fur was sleek, as if oiled. Out the window, rain drilled a band of lawn beyond which stood a squat, redbrick apartment building. She herself appeared to be on the third floor of a house, a Victorian house: the old sash windows, the high ceilings and baseboards.

A man and a dog exited the rear of the apartment building. The man wore a red anorak. His dog, a beagle, had the long teats of a nursing mother. Rose wondered about the puppies, how many there were and what had become of them. She got the impression that Harriet was wondering the same thing. She extinguished her cigarette and crossed to the cupboards. All there was in the cupboard she opened was a tub of Smarties and a bottle of Keen's mustard. She took out the Smarties and ate them in a tranced sort of way.

A buzzer sounded. She held a Smartie at her mouth. The buzzer sounded again, and she dropped the Smartie in the tub and went out to the hall. She pushed the speaker button. "Yes?"

"It's me," said a man.

Her heart leapt, then sank. She leaned her forehead against the doorframe.

"Can I come up?"

She pushed the button again. She opened the door. There was the quick, light step of someone taking the stairs two at a time.

He saw her and halted. He wore a Dodgers ball cap, olive-brown chinos, and a tan T-shirt. He carried a dripping black umbrella. He looked taller to Rose than he'd looked at Goldfinch, his skin paler. He was a tall pale man with a large, distinguished head, like royalty from another century. The sight of him agonized Harriet. "What are you doing here?" she said.

His eyes sprinted up and down her body. "Were you asleep?" He climbed the last few stairs. "Are you alone?"

"See for yourself."

He set his umbrella on her shoe mat. In three strides he was at the entrance to the living room. He swung around. "I don't know what you want." He made the stiff-fingered, gathering motion rappers make, and Rose

123

revised his age downward a couple of years. "Just tell me what you want."

She shut the door. "What I want . . ." Her voice cracked, and she started over. "What I want is for you not to have told me you were separated from Lesley."

"We *were*, technically. A trial separation."

"You made me think it was for good. You only said yesterday it was a trial."

"I just—"

"What I want is for you not to have told me that every time you leave here you're so psyched, you go home and jump Lesley."

"That was . . ." He took off the cap. "It isn't even true. Yeah, I'm psyched from you and me, but I don't have sex with her. She's out to here." He indicated a huge belly.

Did he know that Harriet was pregnant? Rose doubted it. Nothing about his or Harriet's demeanor indicated such knowledge, and, in fact, Harriet, pulling on her hands, seemed to be resisting the temptation to cup her own belly. "So you lie to me," she said sadly.

He shook his head.

"Do you tell Lesley you love her?"

"No."

"When she asks if you love her, what do you say?"

"She doesn't ask."

"She's afraid to."

"Could be."

"I hate this."

"I'm sorry, babe."

She shrank from him. "Don't call me babe."

"Do you want me to go?"

"Yes."

He tried to kiss her. She jerked away. He nuzzled her neck and touched her face. His fingers smelled of oranges. He kissed her. She went limp. Inside her, Rose went limp, and inside Rose another woman seemed to go limp, and then another, inward and smaller, a nested gang of swooning women.

He helped her get her T-shirt off. She lay on the rag rug, and he stripped and knelt beside her. "Yes," he said, surveying her like a man in possession of a nice plank of wood.

He tugged down her underpants and licked the inside of her thighs. He kissed the flesh around her sensitive nipples. He kissed her rib cage, her belly. A twinkling light came on under each place. She stuffed his shirt beneath her head to watch, turning Rose and all the nested women into voyeurs. Rose had a mental image of the twinkling lights and their filaments and braided green wires. She's an alien, she thought. It made sense. It answered everything: the

125

overamped nervous system, this unearthly pleasure now spreading from the center of her body in concentric waves.

The orgasm brought Rose back to Harriet's flesh and blood with a wrench, like grief. He nudged his penis into her mouth, and she held it hand-over-hand. At the point of ejaculation he entered her. He came in silence, a thousand miles away, Rose felt, from Harriet and even himself.

They lay on their backs. "Well, that was something," he said.

Harriet's spirits were already plunging.

"You're so unbelievably fit," he said. He put his arm around her, and she stroked the craters and stubble that were his acne scars and bristle. She seemed stranded there, in that no-man's-land.

"We're acting out Lesley's worst fear," she said.

"What's the time?" He twisted his watch around.

"We're monsters," she said.

"Twelve thirty."

"What if I was pregnant?"

"You're on the pill."

"It isn't foolproof. Especially if you miss a day." She raised herself to see his expression.

"You missed a day?"

She held up two fingers.

"You missed *two* days?"

She nodded.

"So you're saying you're pregnant?"

"Do I look pregnant?" She was truly curious.

Tell him, Rose thought.

He glanced down at her body.

"Don't look at my breasts. Look at my face. Is this the face of a pregnant woman?"

"What are you doing, Harriet?"

Tell him.

She slumped onto her back. "Fucking with you."

"Okay, you just scared the crap out of me. Jesus."

She nibbled at her fingernails for any bit she could get her teeth into. Rose had never chewed her own nails, but chewing Harriet's she felt the solace of a great need being met. David said "Jesus" again. From outside came the occasional sizzle of a passing car.

"I should take the job in London," she said.

"Didn't you turn them down?"

"The trouble is I've developed this fear of flying, of being crammed in. They'd have to pay for a suite on an ocean liner."

"You'd hate London, it's—" The buzzer cut him off. "Are you expecting someone?"

"No."

They waited. It buzzed again.

"Aren't you going to answer?"

"No."

Through the floor they heard the faint noise of another intercom.

"It's for downstairs," she said.

"There should be names under those doorbells," he said.

"Why would I hate London?"

He relaxed. "There's no room. Talk about being crammed in. You'd never find a place this size."

His buoyant tone hurt Harriet. "I don't need a place this size."

"They might put you up somewhere. You could write it into your contract. Accommodation demands, so many square feet."

"You sound like you want me to go."

"I don't want you to go anywhere." He patted her stomach. She rolled into him, and he kissed her, and Rose felt it all starting again, the weakness, the sinking.

But then he tensed. There was a noise in the stairwell, footsteps slowly thudding up. "Is that coming here?" he asked.

She moved out of his arms. "Shh."

Something fell right outside, some solid, light thing. The person knocked. They stayed still. The person knocked again, harder. David gave his head an impatient scratch.

"Harriet!" the person called. "It's Lesley Novak!"

"Fuck," David mouthed.

They began to gather their clothes.

"Your downstairs neighbor said you were home!"

David was as white as his socks. "Bedroom?" he mouthed.

"Office." She tiptoed after him. She opened the closet, took out a green denim dress, and pulled it over her head.

David hopped around, trying to get his foot through his pant leg. "That's her umbrella," he whispered.

"It's black." Harriet was alarmed, but his greater alarm steadied her. "It's generic."

"What's she doing here?"

"The baby clothes, I don't know."

"Christ."

"Shh. Don't move."

Lesley was sitting against the banister, her legs stretched out, her hands resting on a soccer-ball-sized belly. Harriet felt a flustering ache of pity, and stepped forward. "There should be a chair here. Are you okay?"

The black umbrella—it must have been what had fallen—lay on the ground. A dripping blue-and-green-plaid umbrella hung from the railing. "You took your time," Lesley said in a friendly enough voice.

"Sorry. I was in the bathroom. You should have called."

"I don't have your number." Her hair was black. Her eyes were large and heavy-lidded under thick brows. "I only know the address because Clayton used to live here."

"Oh, that's right."

"I was driving by." She made a move to stand.

"Can I help you?"

She slid forward until she was lying on her back. "I'm fine, I do this every day," she said and turned on her side and raised herself to her hands and knees. A long, narrow ponytail like an extension cord hung over her shoulder. She lifted her hands and went into a squat. She adjusted her stance.

All this activity was making Harriet uncomfortable. "Did you come for the baby clothes?" she asked. "I was going to bring them to work on Monday. Is David in on Monday? Well, it doesn't matter, I can leave them in his office. Are you sure you're okay?"

Lesley pushed off from her knees, and then she was standing. "Going down," she panted, "is not a problem."

"Come in. Please."

"Let me catch my breath." She was as slight as Harriet but differently slight: unmuscled, soft. Her arms, now that they were out of service, hung from her sleeveless sundress. She shuffled through the open door and headed for the living room. "I'd kill for a glass of water. Sparkling, if you have it."

"I have Perrier. With ice?"

"Sure. Thanks."

In the kitchen Harriet's composure faltered. She tipped the bottle too far forward, and water galloped out and missed the glass. She relit her cigarette, took a deep drag, extinguished it.

Lesley had chosen a wingback chair between pillars of cardboard boxes. She looked enthroned, a fertility goddess. "I remember your place on Glen Manor," she said, accepting her drink. "You hosted a launch for like two hundred people."

"That must have been, what, five years ago?"

"Anyway, about the baby clothes."

"Right. So, there's everything. Booties, sleepers, dresses, little shirts and pants."

"How old are your friend's kids?"

"Old now, in their late teens."

"Why did she save their clothes?"

"She's a pack rat, but she's downsizing into a condo, so. They're in excellent condition. I could get them now if you want. Did you drive?"

Lesley was gulping her drink. She drained the glass. "I perspire gallons," she said.

"Would you like a refill?"

"No, thanks." She chewed a piece of ice. "The thing is," she said, "we don't need more clothes."

"Oh, you don't?"

"I've had three baby showers."

Harriet was uneasy. She perched on the edge of the sofa. "David didn't say."

"I guess he wanted to include you somehow. And you wanted to give me something so you wouldn't feel so guilty."

"Sorry?"

"About the affair." She spoke plainly, almost sympathetically. "Is he here? I thought I heard something."

"No," she said. But Harriet was stunned. She was beaten. "Yes," she said dimly.

"He's here."

"Yes."

"Well, let's leave him where he is for the moment."

"Lesley, listen I—"

"If you don't mind, Harriet, I'd like *you* to listen. First, I'm not leaving him. If he leaves me, that's his choice. Second, I think you should know you aren't—"

☍

A cough that started in Harriet's throat ended in Rose's. She was hunched over her desk, still gripping the padded hanger. She was crying. She put the hanger on the phone book and gazed around to establish her surroundings: the Wall of Stars, the sofa, the DVDs. She felt as if she'd been in Harriet for a month.

I think you should know you aren't what? The first? Perhaps David was a habitual philanderer, and Lesley's message was, "You're one in a long line." This would help explain her saintly calm.

But the really startling thing for Rose was the revelation of how much Ava and Harriet were alike, especially their eyes. Of all the people in the world, was Harriet the person Rose entered because of her eyes?

She went to the sofa and lay down and surrendered to thinking about her sister deliberately and fully, as she'd spent the past twenty-three years trying *not* to think about her. She let images of Ava enter her body and leave, enter and leave. At one particular image she paused: Ava holding a jigsaw-puzzle piece between her thumb and forefinger, the other fingers lifted, her features skewered with a misgiving that reminded Rose of Harriet looking up from the sink.

Had Harriet looked up at Rose's urging? Was Rose getting through to her? Later, with David, Harriet had said, "I've *developed* this fear of flying, of being crammed in." God, what if Rose was getting through to her so deeply she was introducing Ava's neuroses?

She wondered about her own mind, then, whether it entered the episodes unscathed or, the opposite, whether it carried off something precious: maternal instinct, for example. She had yet to feel the fetus move, but then she probably wouldn't—that is to say, Harriet wouldn't—this early on. Rose had certainly felt everything else. The orgasm. Although *had* she felt the orgasm? On her own, here in her chair? Was the husk of her body able to feel anything?

She looked at her watch. One thirty-five. David would have been called into the discussion by now. She could just see him standing between Harriet and Lesley, sheepish, turning his ball cap in his hands. Regardless of what he said, Rose felt sure that, for Harriet, the affair was over. The scene itself might be over, David and Lesley gone, Harriet alone. *Call someone*, Rose thought, hoping to transmit if not the words, then the impulse. Her eyes were blinking shut. She was very tired.

Call your sister, she thought. *Or Marsh. Call Marsh. Marry Marsh. He loves you.*

☉

When Fiona didn't answer the phone, Rose presumed she'd already left. Either that or she'd forgotten about the grocery shopping and was still gardening. Now, a third possibility presented itself: Fiona on the front porch, annoyed, tapping her watch.

"I lost track of the time," Rose said, winded. She'd run most of the way.

Fiona came to her feet. "Ava, darling, is that you?" she said in her brogue.

Rose stopped. "It's Rose."

"Who?"

"Rose."

"Where's Ava?"

Was some Ava-like aspect clinging to her? "There's only me, Mom."

"Why do you call me Mom?"

"I'm your other daughter. Rose. You gave birth to me in 1971."

"That date means nothing to me," Fiona said. But her face cleared, and in her normal voice she said, "We're late," and moved decisively down the steps to the driver's side of the car.

"Mom, I'll drive."

"I'm driving, I can drive."

"Your glasses."

"Oh, yes, where are they?"

"Around your neck."

Before Rose had her seat belt on, they were reversing at high speed. "Slow down," Rose said. They bolted across the street. "Brake!" she cried. The car bumped over the curb. "Push right to the floor!" she cried, and Fiona did, although too late for Caroline's ornamental juniper.

In the ensuing silence Fiona's breath whistled.

"Turn off the engine," Rose said.

Fiona turned it off.

"Get out of the car. Leave the keys."

Fiona obeyed. Rose climbed out and inspected the bumper. Among the old scratches and dents, any fresh damage was camouflaged. She got back in, drove onto the road, and parked.

"We'll replace it!" she called to Charles, who was making his deliberate, erect way down the lawn. The tree was basically a narrow trunk supporting an oversized globe of foliage. It had always looked as if it might keel over, and now it had.

"Mrs. Bowan," Charles said to Fiona in the dulcet voice that must have found favor with the officials he once squired around Mombasa, "assure me that you are not hurt."

"We just had the engine overhauled," Fiona said.

"Ah! Mechanical failure."

"The car's fine," said Rose. "And we're fine, thanks. But the poor tree."

"Junipers never flourish in direct sunlight," Fiona said. "I told Caroline that the day she bought it."

Charles bent over, clutching his thighs and in so doing betraying them to be gaunt under the generous drape of his trousers. He lifted the trunk and tottered. Rose reached to help, but he clasped the tree possessively and after a few rickety steps brought it upright.

"Now then," he said.

"Did Caroline get it from Sheridan's?" Rose asked.

He didn't seem to hear.

"I'll ask her," Rose said. To her mother she said, "We can buy another one tomorrow."

"What will that set us back?" Fiona wanted to know.

"My dear ladies," Charles intervened, "I believe we have reason to hope. Take it, Rose, if you would." And he relinquished the tree and walked to the side door of his house and went in.

"Where's he going?" said Fiona.

"To get something," Rose said irritably. Her mother wasn't cheap, but at times like this Rose had to wonder. Maybe she *was* cheap, she'd always been cheap, and now that her surface graces were beginning to wear thin, her essential cheapness was shining through.

Charles returned with duct tape, a ball of green string, a pair of scissors, and a broom handle.

"We were hoping to get the shopping done," Fiona said.

Charles dropped the tape, string, and scissors. "This will be quick," he said and moved up against the base of the tree. He raised the broom handle high, staggered backward, and thrust it into the earth.

The taping of the gash and the tying of the sapling he entrusted to Rose, under his supervision. He said that the arthritis in his fingers had progressed to the point where he could no longer tie a knot. He held them out, and they were like antlers. "Otherwise," he said, addressing Fiona, "I'm as fit as a fiddle."

"If this doesn't work, we'll replace it," Rose said yet again.

He turned to her. His bloodshot eyes were the oldest living things she'd ever seen. "Let us think positively," he said.

In the car (Rose at the wheel, no argument), Fiona took issue with his fit-as-a-fiddle remark. "What do I care? Anyway, you don't have to be Superman to shove a pole into a wet lawn."

Rose stirred herself to say, "He shoved it pretty far down." She was brooding over Harriet. She was thinking that Harriet would be leaning toward abortion more than ever, and that she must have gotten those baby clothes from her friend *before* she found out about her own pregnancy. *Well, they're yours now*, Rose thought, as though a bunch of sleepers and booties and little shirts might make a difference. In theory, Rose stood by a woman's dominion over her body. So why did she have this devouring need for Harriet to keep the baby? Because it was as if Ava were pregnant? Because the baby might have Ava's eyes?

"It won't live," said Fiona.

Rose looked over wildly. "What?"

"The tree. It's a goner."

☉

After putting the groceries away, they drove to the theater. Fiona decided to start her annual cleaning of the seat arms, and she entered the auditorium with her dustcloths and lemon oil. Rose escaped upstairs with a box of Smarties. For what felt like the hundredth time she checked that no more storms were expected before tomorrow.

She opened the windows. She lit a cigarette. I've got to work, I'm falling behind, she thought. She never fell behind, it wasn't like her, not the old her, anyway. She listened to phone messages and read comments on the Regal's website. Most of the comments were reviews and didn't require her to weigh in, but she did. It was the sort of thing she could do in her sleep. Everybody was so friendly and knowledgeable. Except—who was this guy? ReelMan9. ReelMan9 was bawling her out for showing tonight's first feature, *Easy Rider*, during Henry Fonda week. "Peter is not Henry," he bristled.

"He isn't?" she muttered. What she typed, copying a paragraph from the Regal's mission statement, was, "The challenge of featuring an artist a week is that four-teen different movies are too many for even the great-est actors to carry. Our solution is to spice things up with compatible classics." To this she added, "*Easy Rider* and *The Grapes of Wrath* work well together, I think: the Fondas, the road trips through the southwestern US, the condemnations of the American Dream."

She gnawed on her thumb. She was in the grip of a savage oral craving, and neither the cigarettes nor the Smarties were satisfying it. She decided to set ReelMan9 even straighter: "Many of our double bills were paired by my father. His programming was gutsy, original, and often just plain whimsical. The reason he paired *It's a Wonderful Life* with *The Party* was that in both movies there are retractable swimming pools. Or take this Sunday's double bill, *The Seven Year Itch* and *Rear Window*. Aside from the similarities of period (mid-1950s), location (Lower Manhattan), weather (heat wave), and plot driver (middle-aged professional white male obsesses over neighbor), both are set in apartments improbably humble for the kinds of salaries a world-famous photojournalist and a successful book editor would have earned back then. I will be writing more about his programming in a future issue of *Coming Attractions*."

Feeling better now, soothed by her mental vacation from Harriet, she reached for the Smarties. The box was empty. She contemplated getting another, but she could smell lasagna warming in the microwave.

Lloyd was seated at the table, and he and Fiona were discussing dance crazes. For the sake of coming across as somebody *not* having an affair, Rose let her mother drop a brick-sized slab of lasagna on her plate. Fiona said, "I can do the twist, I used to do the twist all the time." She put down the spatula and demonstrated. She was all elbows and enthusiasm. Lloyd laughed and sang the let's-do-the-twist song in his gravelly bass.

Don't kill yourself, Rose begged Harriet, thinking how Harriet had only just started taking her antidepressants, if she'd started at all. *Don't kill your baby.*

SEPTEMBER 1982–JUNE 1999

Ava's papier-mâché parrot, Tobikumu, gazed sightlessly toward the window. He had been a Christmas present from a great-uncle who had lived for several years in Tokyo. Rose had gotten Kazuyuki, a delicate papier-mâché cellist with elongated fingers resting on fine strings that might have been dental floss. One day she'd taken him to the house of a new Japanese friend, and there, within five minutes, the friend's poodle had torn him to confetti.

Under Ava's care, Tobikumu, the parrot, stayed perfect. Under Rose's, he lost his glass eyes. She put him on her bedside table so that before falling asleep she could look at his sockets and recover the guilt she'd shed during the day, in those moments when she'd been lighthearted or animated or—the most bewildering offense—pleased

143

with herself. She thought of the guilt as survivor's guilt, and of survivor's guilt as a guilt necessary for survival. Tobikumu was her victim and accuser both. She counted on him to get her to cry herself to sleep.

She cried secretly, in near silence. Still, her parents saw her misery and sent her to a child psychologist, an old woman who was half deaf and therefore needed to sit next to Rose on the sofa. Rose didn't mind. Dr. Grewal's baked-bread grandmotherly smell and her cracked brown face like dried mud were unthreatening and a little heartbreaking. She spoke in a soft, accented voice. She had a tendency to repeat Rose's answers, for both their sakes, Rose understood, in order that Rose might hear them said back to her, and that Dr. Grewal might verify she'd heard them correctly. Rose never mentioned Tobikumu, and when the subject came around to Ava, she said what any normal girl getting better would say: Yes, I'm still sad. No, not as sad as I was. Yes, I understand it wasn't my fault. Mostly they dwelt on Rose's present circumstances, her friends and school, her shyness. To distract Dr. Grewal from asking about Ava, Rose made her shyness sound like a more serious problem than it was. Year after year, as Dr. Grewal's deafness worsened and she sat ever closer, Rose offered up the minor troubles and triumphs of her week.

She would have continued with the therapy indefinitely, but Dr. Grewal retired. This was around the time of Rose's sixteenth birthday and another change in her life: the birth control pill, which she began taking for her period cramps and which had the unexpected side effects of clearing up her acne and enlarging her already large breasts.

Boys at school and men in trucks gave her second looks. She hated this kind of attention, it drove her to walk around hunched and hugging herself. So badly did she want to blend in, however, to escape from the conspicuous clump of girls who had no hope of finding a boyfriend into the wider, less glaring company of those who at least stood a chance, she went out with the first boy who asked.

He was the frighteningly intelligent and cynical editor of the school newspaper, whose political page she had recently supplied with a caricature of Prime Minister Brian Mulroney. They went to see the movie *Raising Arizona* and shared a box of Skittles. Afterward, they were taking a shortcut to the subway when he began shivering spasmodically.

"It's my blood vessels," he said and lurched behind a Shoppers Drug Mart dumpster. "They get restricted, and I feel like I'm freezing to death."

She offered him her jacket. He was about her size.

"No, thanks," he said. "Believe it or not ..." He laughed weakly. "This will sound like a joke."

"What?"

"Ejaculation helps."

"Pardon?"

"It gets my blood pumping." He unzipped his pants.

Such an obvious lie. So stupid and stunning. If she stalked off, he'd see how fat her bum looked in her new jeans. She turned her head and stared at a plastic bag between the dumpster and the brick wall, and he reached for her hand and got her started. Once he'd established a vigorous stroke, he let her carry on alone. She was aware of him groaning and of tears smudging her vision. Just before he came, he grabbed his penis and aimed away from their legs. "Thanks," he said, tucking it in his pants. "I feel a lot better."

"I have to buy some . . ." she said. She went in the rear entrance of the drugstore and walked through and out the front.

He avoided her at school. She told her girlfriends, "We didn't click." There was no possibility of telling them what had happened, and not because it was disgusting, although it was, in a puny, pathetic way (less so to her than it would have been to them), but because she had gotten her hopes up. She had wanted more, and he had rightly shamed her.

She wasn't asked out again until her second year of university. By then she was ready to believe that Ava would have wanted her to live a normal life. The belief didn't liberate her or console her as much as point her toward what she imagined a normal life entailed.

It was the end of term, a party in a frat house. She arrived late and had to step over bodies and squeeze past lunging drunks to reach the kitchen. An older, slouching guy with longish hair and clever eyes handed her a beer. "Let's make a break for it," he said.

They walked to a park and sat at a picnic table. He wasn't the professor she took him to be from his age and vocabulary. He had master's degrees in philosophy and political science but the only job he'd been able to find was telemarketer. "I get hung up on an average of twenty times an hour," he said cheerfully. Then he said, "Let's not talk about that, let's talk about your gorgeous arms. Hold them out."

She did, tentatively.

"All the way out."

She extended them farther.

"I adore them," he said.

He challenged her to an arm wrestle. She let him win. "It's all technique, really," he said and launched into an explanation of top roll versus hook, hand size versus wrist endurance, and other such considerations. She took this to be slightly inebriated chatter.

It wasn't. It was who he was, what he did. It was his university degrees in action. When they decided to have sex for the first time, while they were still drinking tequila shots (another first for her), he paced the bedroom of her flat and listed the pros and cons of her losing her virginity to a man in the midst of reformulating his concept of romantic love.

Her ears were chiming. At last she removed all her clothes and got in under the covers. She had worked hard—as hard as he was working now—to talk herself into this. Not the losing her virginity part, but rather the right, the *obligation*, to experience the pleasure it promised.

"Okay, I'm going to sleep," she said.

"What the hell," he said and jumped on her.

He knew his way around her body. But Rose could maintain a state of excitement only if she imagined him at work, being hung up on. She faked her orgasm.

By all measures, except for her inability to come, their sex was torrid—extended foreplay, every possible position. Afterward, he would hold her tight and debate both sides of some topic, it could be anything. He seemed to think from her shifts and sighs that she was listening and contributing. In fact, she was silently debating both sides of the frigidity issue. Was faking your orgasm an act of generosity or of selfishness? Was frigidity a physical or temperamental condition? Did she want to be frigid? Was frigidity a source of power for her or a shrine to her everlasting guilt?

Eight months into the relationship he told her as nicely as such things can be told, but unequivocally, no beating around the bush, that he was seeing a woman on Canada's Olympic rowing team.

She stayed single for two years. This was during the time of her father's diagnosis and then his death, and she was working seven days a week. Also, her bad periods had returned, with more blood and pain than ever. Some days it was all she could do to climb the theater stairs. She postponed seeing a doctor in case she, too, had a fatal illness, her fear being not so much that she would die but that her mother would be left alone.

It wasn't cancer, it was fibroids. The gynecologist said he could remove them, but she would grow more. She asked if she needed a hysterectomy.

"It's an option," he said.

She had just buried her father. She couldn't afford to spend days bleeding and writhing in bed. And to tell the truth, she'd been expecting something like this since the day Ava died. A big reckoning, a penance. Only in the recovery room did it really hit her that she would never be able to *bear* children. She could have them, adopt them, but she couldn't bear them. She had told Fiona that any new fibroids were likely to be malignant, and she decided to believe this herself. Although she didn't really.

Fiona blamed the fibroids on overwork. She said she knew of other young women who had spoiled their female plumbing by working themselves ragged. Right there in the hospital she ruled that they were going to cancel the matinees.

"Really?" Rose said. The matinees had been beloved by her father.

"They're money losers," Fiona said, a fact she had refused to acknowledge before now. "What are we?" she said. "A charity?"

So now Rose had Saturday and Sunday afternoons to herself. She began meeting friends at cafés. She attended art openings and saw first-run movies.

One Sunday afternoon she went to a fund-raiser for the National Ballet and found herself seated next to a composer and music teacher recently arrived from Hong Kong. Marlin Lau. While everybody else at their table ignored the two of them, they discovered a mutual interest in Japanese cinema. He liked the later films of Kurosawa, the rest he called "missteps." Rose had been taught by her father to revere Kurosawa, and the fact that Marlin Lau could write off *The Seven Samurai* with one withering word gave her a strange thrill. So did the way he looked: slender and elegant, but with a strong concave face, like the man in the moon. On his ring finger he wore a gold band. Was his wife here in Toronto? Rose asked.

He tapped his napkin to his lips. "I am a widower."

"Oh, I'm sorry."

He gave a slight bow. He reminded Rose of Alec Guinness playing the formal Japanese widower in *A Majority of One*. A cross between Alec Guinness and Kazuyuki, her papier-mâché cellist.

The similarities turned out to be skin-deep (or paper-thin, as she would one day tell the story). Marlin was sensitive only insofar as everything offended him, every sort of fashion, any sort of trend or variation on a theme. Any *theme*. If he could name it or name its antecedent, it was derivative and therefore worthless. Months had to pass for Rose to appreciate the scope of his disdain let alone recognize it *as* disdain rather than principled intelligence. He had no friends, and he didn't think much of hers.

But three mornings a week, in the apartment he sublet on St. Clair West, he did something with his musician's fingers, and she had an orgasm, a fleeting tremor, a reflex that had nothing to do with love on her part, or even lust. To bring herself to lie down in the first place, she had to think about his dead wife and his stalled career. As far as she could tell, his compositions were performed only by his students. His Symphony no. 1 in G Minor had been in the works for fifteen years.

She would never love him, but she wanted him to love her. The man you were with was supposed to love you. Besides, he had loved his wife and often told her so.

Then one morning she stopped caring whether he loved her or not. She went to sleep caring and woke up asking herself, what am I doing? Apart from the strain of listening to his countless specific and indefinite resentments, there was the fact that he preferred to see her midmorning, during those hours when, normally, she would be having breakfast and doing household chores. But how do you break up with a lonely, recent-immigrant widower?

To celebrate his first year in Toronto she took him to a new four-star luncheon bistro called Les Trois Cloches. They rarely ate out (neither of them could afford it, and his standards were merciless), so when he examined his menu without wincing, she was able to sit back and read her own. Scarcely above a murmur she sang "Les

Trois Cloches," a song she knew from all those after-noons listening to her father play his Édith Piaf records.

"Please stop," Marlin said.

"Oh." She looked around. "Was that too loud?"

"No."

Was she off-key? She couldn't bear to ask.

"You sing through your nasal passages."

Worse than off-key. "God. Sorry."

"You are untrained."

"Why didn't you tell me before?"

"When should I have told you?"

"Sunday?" While trying to figure out his German coffeemaker, she had sung "Edelweiss." "How long have I been torturing you? God."

"Please keep your voice down."

"My voice *is* down." Or was it? She had lost all confidence in her voice.

He straightened his cutlery. "I have something to say to you. It was my intention to wait until the dessert course."

"I chew with my mouth open?" she tried joking.

He went still, either at the indelicacy or the realization. Back to business, he rotated his plate an inch. "I feel very strongly that you and I have reached, if you will forgive the jargon, our sell-by date."

"As a couple?" she asked, hardly daring to hope.

"We lack compatibility." He flicked a speck of dust from the plate. "We have lacked it from the beginning, if we are honest with each other."

"From the get-go," she said a little too eagerly. She lowered her eyes. "I mean, I actually like *The Seven Samurai*."

"We have different aspirations."

"We live in different worlds."

"I need . . ." He folded his hands on the edge of the table. "I want . . ."

He wanted to finish his symphony, she thought, moved. She reached across and placed a hand over his.

"I very much want . . ."

"I know," she said.

"To have children," he said.

℗

She swore off men. Who needed them? Who had the time? Victor was a blind date, and she agreed to go out with him only because she hadn't dated anyone in five years, and his father had died a few months earlier.

They met for lunch. Like a certain type of intelligent man he imparted facts as a way of holding up his side of the conversation. But his facts were entertaining and always related to whatever they'd been talking about. Neither she nor her mother could bring herself to kill an ant, she said, and he said an ant dragging a moth through a lawn was equivalent, in terms of strength, to a man lifting a light aircraft through a bamboo grove. They both noticed how white their server's teeth were, and he said that ancient Romans cleaned their teeth with urine. She learned that a shoreline is infinite because it is infinitely jagged, and that Graham Greene wouldn't have written *The Power and the Glory* if he hadn't escaped to Mexico after publishing a review in which he accused Shirley Temple's most ardent admirers of being licentious clergymen.

By dessert Victor's wandering eye seemed less an endearing affliction than a consequence of such wide-ranging interests. They were discussing the illegitimate progeny of movie stars, and Rose, knowing she would see him again, confessed to being infertile. "It was a deal breaker with my last boyfriend," she said.

"The composer?" Victor said, evidently having heard of him through their mutual friend. "Well, it would be a deal *maker* with me."

"You don't like kids?"

"Drooling, incontinent lunatics. Not really."

She laughed, relieved but a bit disturbed. It wasn't that she didn't like children.

"Most of them grow into passable humans," he said. "Eventually. Unless they're male."

He was only trying to separate himself from Marlin Lau, she told herself. "Some males grow out of it," she said and smiled at him. "I hope."

He smiled back. "A few of us do."

FRIDAY, JULY 1, 2005

Rose began to record the episodes so far.

First she drew a diagram of Harriet's apartment. She outlined the doors, windows, appliances, furniture, bookshelves, sinks, toilet, and bathtub. Where she had noticed them, she added the overhead lights, light switches, plants, and unpacked boxes. She shaded in colors. She drew the calico cat on the bed and the black-and-white cat on the windowsill.

She then created a computer file and chronicled everything that had happened, including word-for-word dialogue, as nearly as she could recapture it. She described Harriet's physical sensations and her emotions, these latter being the tricky part, whether to go with frustration or disappointment, dread or dismay. She felt a powerful sense of responsibility, far beyond the one she owed her future, potentially skeptical self, to be her miracle's exemplary witness.

Downstairs, *Easy Rider* ended, intermission came and went, and *The Grapes of Wrath* started. During the scene where Ma Joad is crying, "We got a sick old lady!" Rose saved the computer file with the name "Being Harriet Smith" and closed her eyes.

"Wake up," her mother said.

"Did you knock?" Rose asked, sitting up.

"I always knock."

"It must have been the heavy meal."

Fiona let that go, but in the car she said, "When I was pregnant with you, I slept on my feet."

"I'm not pregnant," said Rose. "And I'm not having an affair, either."

"Who said you were having an affair?"

"I can't be pregnant."

"Why not?"

It wasn't that the memories Fiona mislaid were unimportant to her. If only that were the case, if only she were able to hang on to what she cherished most, like a person grabbing the birdcage and photo albums before running out of a burning house. Rose understood how blameless her mother was, but she was tired, and she said, "Mom, think about it."

They had pulled into their driveway. Rose glanced over.

"No," Fiona murmured, "that doesn't work."

"I forget myself sometimes," Rose said, sorry now that she had pressed.

"You'll never be a mother," Fiona said.

"Not a biological one, no."

Moths dithered around their porch light. Fiona watched them and chewed her bottom lip. Did she realize she was home?

"So I'll see you in the morning," Rose said.

Fiona didn't budge. She said, "When I stare blankly, I'm not blank. I'm concentrating."

"Okay," Rose said.

"I think it must be the same with old people in wheelchairs and hospital beds, the people who get written off, when their minds are years and years away, concentrating on a few minutes that they're the only ones in the world who remember."

"Nobody writes you off," Rose said.

"I don't mean a birthday or a conversation. I mean an *atmosphere*. An atmosphere when I was so alive that I noticed everything around me. The atmosphere around me." She looked at Rose.

"The weather," Rose suggested. "The light."

"Everything all blended together. Whatever it is that makes an atmosphere. Lately I've been trying to get back the atmosphere from a winter morning, oh, fifty years ago, it must have been. I'd just met your father, and I was head over heels in love. I was on my way to my job at Tip Top Tailors." Her hand encircled the cuff of her blouse. At Tip Top Tailors she had sewn shirt cuffs. "It was Christmastime. It was snowing. There was snow on the window ledges. The fruit stands had navel oranges in towers, bunches of mistletoe, and holly tied with red ribbon. I was wearing a green velvet beret, tilted to one side, like a French girl." She demonstrated adjusting such a hat.

"I'll bet Dad liked it," Rose said with a full heart.

"He liked my ankles," Fiona said. She picked up her purse and opened her door. "Off you go," she said, "wherever it is you go."

Rose took the Lake Shore to avoid construction. She lowered her window so that Victor wouldn't smell the cigarette smoke on her clothes, even as she asked herself what business it was of his if she smoked. To her left Lake Ontario was a gray vacancy beyond fogged-in condo towers and strips of parkland. Puddles the size of ponds almost dragged the car to a halt.

At Victor's she let herself into the foyer, but then she just stood there. The living room clock struck the midnight hour. Why wasn't she with her mother, who would never be a grandmother and who was not incapable of mistaking a can of oven cleaner for a can of air freshener? Why wasn't she searching for the apartment building she'd seen from Harriet's window?

Victor appeared as if out of a mist, on the other side of the glass door. "I thought I heard something," he said. "I've opened a really nice Shiraz."

She followed him to the kitchen.

"Is there a word for the parents of a dead child?" she asked. They were on their second glass of wine. "The parental equivalent of *orphan*?"

He took a sip of his wine. "I don't think so. We've got *widow*, *widower*."

"It's too horrible to have a word."

"We've got the adjectives," he said. "*Bereaved*, *grieving*." Although he knew, of course, that Ava had died, he didn't make the connection to *her* parents and *their* dead child, but talked about how the English language had all these gaps. Where was the word for the feeling of being alone in the woods? The Germans had one: *Waldeinsamkeit*. Or the word for apprehending your own misery? The Czechs had one. "But then," he said, "they would."

Rose looked at the plaid wallpaper his mother must have thought was so modern and North American when she'd picked it out. Where was the word for a man who hated children and had almost put his agoraphobic mother in a nursing home?

They went to the bedroom. That was what they did after the wine and cheese. She undressed and lay beside him and hoped it wouldn't take too long. But as they kissed, a guilty sense that she had betrayed him with David had her trying harder. And then, when she closed her eyes, he *was* David. She opened her eyes: Victor. Closed them: David.

She kept them closed.

SATURDAY, JULY 2, 2005

Rose phoned Victor and tried to get him to deny Environment Canada's forecast. She had gone to the theater early with the intention of screening DVDs ahead of the storm, but when she arrived and checked the Weather Network, the radar showed the storm tracking north. And now Victor was saying that it would miss downtown altogether.

"I can see the anvil," Rose said.

"Does Fiona have to go somewhere?"

"No. It's just so crazy, all these storms."

"You haven't had any more migraine symptoms, have you?"

"It's not that, I'm not worried. Well, I'm a bit worried about the theater roof."

"We're in the clear until tomorrow mid- to late afternoon."

"There's always the chance of a pop-up later today, right?"

"I'm not calling for a pop-up, no."

Rose got off the phone and spent the next several minutes swallowing convulsively. Being told she would have to wait another day to be with Harriet was like being told she would have to wait another day for a heart transplant.

She considered the hanger, still there on her desk. At some point between Thursday night and this morning she had endowed it with supernatural clout. She took it in both hands and rubbed the silk padding over her skin and prayed for Harriet to be strong and safe and to want the baby. She prayed for the storm to drift south, she motioned the hanger like a hook to snag it near. And then she realized that she could put *herself* near the *storm*.

A quarter of an hour later she was racing up the Don Valley Parkway. She wished she had thought of this sooner. On the radio they were reporting power lines and trees down in the Caledon area. Ahead of her and to the west she could see the yellowish-white anvil spreading out from its lid. At the first sound of thunder, she would pull over. An episode in a parked car would be as safe as one in her office. Safer, really, with the risk of discovery all but eliminated.

South of Highway 407 she met a band of rain. There was no lightning, though, no thunder. For several miles the rain blew sideways, and she followed the barely visible taillights of an SUV. Who were these other drivers? What missions could they possibly be on that they were entrusting their lives to the eyesight and reflexes of the strangers in front of them?

The rain stopped, but the traffic still crawled. Meanwhile, the storm was farther away than it had been fifteen minutes ago. She took the next exit and turned west in hopes of finding a secondary north-south route. She drove well over the limit. There were few other cars, and the road had been widened to accommodate the four-car garages of half-built houses, ranks and ranks abutting the property lines of abandoned fields with their bulky gray barns that for Rose, even in glimpses, were awful.

A red light suspended from wires caught her unawares, and she almost sideswiped a truck. In her mirror she saw blue sky. More alarmed by this than by the near collision, she continued racing until she was slowed again by traffic. The clouds pushed northward. She would never catch them.

She pulled over.

She was next to a field of grazing horses. She lit a cigarette and watched them despondently. Ever since the farm Rose preferred not to look at ponies or horses, but she looked at this herd. Six mares and a foal. What depressed her was their imprisonment, which they themselves might not have minded.

Her thoughts turned to Marsh, who, she remembered, taught a two-thirty yoga class. What was the time? Ten to twelve. If she couldn't have an episode, and she couldn't see Harriet out in the world, maybe she could see Marsh and get him to talk about Harriet. At the very least she could reconfirm her miracle.

☉

The front door was unlocked, the reception desk vacant. She went to the changing room and searched in her purse for a quarter so that she could open locker number eight. She couldn't find one. What she did find was the card from the cab driver who had offered to make love to her all night long: *Aldo Gatti. Bodybuilder, Women's Companion.* She pinned it to the bulletin board among business cards offering mindfulness therapy and pet sitting. You never knew.

Back in the hall she walked past a number of narrow offices and treatment rooms and came to the larger space where Marsh had held his class. An ancient woman in a coral-colored leotard and tights stood alone by the window and slowly rotated her bottom. Rose felt a pang to think of her mother doing the twist when there was this other, more decorous way for an old woman to swivel her lower body, should she be so inclined. She asked if Marsh was around.

The woman continued her rotations. "Try the kitchen," she said. She pointed a bent finger. "End of the hall."

He was hunkered over an enormous pot, a big man in a little apron. Rose felt faint. That he should exist! That he should *still* exist! And that his attitude of intense absorption should be familiar to her, and lovable. Only now did she think he might not welcome the woman who had pestered him for Harriet's address. But he looked up, and in a tone of warm recognition said, "Oh, hello."

She gestured. "You're cooking."

"My work here is done." He hefted the pot onto another burner. "Spicy turnip-seaweed soup. Would you like some?"

"No, thank you."

"It's not as foul as it sounds." He removed his apron and draped it over one of the many mismatched wooden

167

chairs surrounding an old farmhouse table. She stepped in, light on her feet, ghostly with secret intelligence. Her plan until this moment had been to say she wanted to register for classes, but it was occurring to her that this might involve a deposit or other complications. I think I left my wallet here, she rehearsed. No, too dire.

"I'm sorry, I've forgotten your name," Marsh said.

"Rose."

"Rose, yes. Of course."

"I think I might have left my scarf here."

"I haven't heard of a scarf. But we can check the office."

She followed him out a different door and along a corridor. It was all she could do not to lay a hand on his broad, round-shouldered back. A yoga teacher with round shoulders, you didn't expect it. To Rose it implied a history of heartache and disappointment: an earlier failed career in England, or a divorce, children he'd lost custody of. She wondered if Harriet had told him about being pregnant.

"Did you drop off that manuscript at Goldfinch?" he asked.

"No," she said, startled. "No, not yet. I'm trying to arrange a meeting with Harriet."

"She's a busy woman."

"It's getting past the receptionist. It's like Fort Knox there."

They turned down a second corridor whose low ceiling was scrolled with pipes. He reached up to touch them. "This used to be a glass factory."

She waited for him to address her dilemma, but it seemed he had mentioned the manuscript only for the sake of being polite. "Really," she said.

"I studied glassblowing in my wayward youth. All I remember is the cardinal rule—don't inhale." He took a key from his pocket. "Here we are."

It was a narrow room with windows flanking one side. From a shelf above the desk he lifted a cardboard box and set it down and began rummaging through the contents: single gloves and mittens, a hairbrush, a folded umbrella that disarmed Rose for being the same blue-and-green plaid as the one David's wife had brought to Harriet's.

Marsh tugged out a wool scarf. "Is this it?"

"No."

"The cleaners were here last night. If it isn't here . . ."

He looked at her over his glasses. How could somebody who had described her eyes as soulful not see the fraudulence they must be beaming? She craned her neck as if to search for her scarf in the immediate vicinity. "I must have left it somewhere else."

"Would you settle for this? It's been here longer than I have." He was holding the umbrella.

"Actually, I wouldn't mind some soup after all."

Back down the corridor they went, the umbrella staying with them as a subject of conversation. He said he had left his umbrella at a yoga retreat and might take this one. She recommended he visit the subway lost and found. "All you have to do is say you've lost a black umbrella, and they show you about a hundred, and you pick the nicest."

He laughed. "Isn't that stealing?"

"Isn't taking an umbrella from here stealing?"

"Good point."

They were in the kitchen now, and she sat at the table as he ladled out a single bowl. Because of her diet she declined the bread, although it smelled wonderful.

"How is it?" Marsh asked, sitting across from her.

"Good," she said. In fact, it tasted like dirt. He folded his arms and watched her with such keen interest that she had to look down. She swallowed another spoonful, and a vision came to her of being naked and stretched out on the table, and the yoga people—that ancient woman from down the hall, the woman at the party with the buzz cut, the guy who'd made the flower-show joke—all of them chanting like the devil worshippers in *Rosemary's Baby*. In the real world Marsh was saying that every day one of the staff threw together a vegan soup or stew for anybody who wanted it. "I eat here two, three times a week," he said, standing to get a bowl of soup for himself. Rose's vision evaporated. Oh, she was paranoid! Ridiculous!

They ate in silence, but he kept glancing at her and smiling, trying to place her outside of Thursday's encounter, she guessed, and she wondered if there were things about her that reminded him of Harriet: her jumpy nerves, and the cigarette smoke she herself could smell in her hair, but also imperceptible things connected to her brief sharing of Harriet's body and emotions. Hadn't she surprised even herself with her sympathy for the horses?

Horses. She stopped eating and got her purse from the chair next to her. "Do you know the Regal Theater?" she asked.

"The rep place? Up on Mount Pleasant?"

"I own it," she said, unzipping her purse. "My mother and I do."

"So that's who you are!"

"You've been, then."

"Recently. I saw *The Hustler*, when was it? Three, four weeks ago. The marvelous woman behind the concession, is she your mother?"

"That's her." Rose withdrew a pair of tickets.

"She asked me if I was Burt Reynolds. She pretended not to believe me when I said I wasn't. I was quite flattered."

"I'm sure she thought you *were* Burt Reynolds. She has dementia."

"Oh." He put his spoon down. "I'm terribly sorry."

"You couldn't know. It's not the first time she's done it is all. One of our regulars has a thyroid condition, and she keeps asking her if she's Shelley Duvall."

Why was she telling him this? To gain his sympathy and trust, that's why. To meet Harriet. "She goes in and out of delusions," she said and handed him the tickets. "Mostly in. So far."

"Regal Theater," he read. "Admit one adult."

"For the soup," she said.

"There's no fee!" He tried giving them back.

"Please take them."

"I couldn't possibly."

"You could. Please."

"I'll take one, then."

"Take them both. Bring a friend."

"Well, thank you. That's very generous."

"We're showing *Hidalgo* and *The Misfits* tonight. So if you're into horses . . ." She almost added, or if you have a friend who's into horses. But from the way he blinked, she got the feeling that Harriet had entered his mind anyway.

"Actually, I'm very much into horses," he said. He placed the tickets on the table near her hand. "But I have something on tonight."

"Oh."

"Would you like more soup?"

"Pardon? No." She slid the tickets back. "Keep them. They're good anytime." It was possible that he might bring Harriet another night. It was just that tonight, when the connection between the features was one of Harriet's favorite animals, the odds of him bringing her were far better. Why had Rose seen the horses in the field if the universe wasn't conspiring on her behalf?

"You've worn me down," he said and put the tickets in his shirt pocket.

He walked her as far as the front door. Even now she was scrambling for the lie that would get him to the theater tonight. All she came up with was, "My mother loves Burt Reynolds. She'll be so happy to see you again."

"I'll work on my American accent," he said.

She drove south to the Lake Shore. At Dufferin she went north and started crisscrossing uptown. She stuck to side streets, since in Harriet's apartment she hadn't

173

heard much traffic. She kept the radio tuned to 680 News for the weather report every ten minutes.

Following a grid turned out to be impossible, however, with most of the streets one-way, and the thoroughfares dead-ended by concrete traffic barriers. Out of frustration she tried convincing herself that a clearly wrong redbrick low-rise was the building she'd seen from Harriet's kitchen window. She stopped in front of the house next door and peered at the top floor. She was like a spurned lover. But this *is* love, she thought. How can I not love someone who reminds me of Ava? How can I not love someone I've been *inside*?

It was late by the time she returned to the theater. She was entering the kitchen when a delivery man from Tasty Thai appeared at the back door. "How much?" she asked.

Fiona got up from the table, where she and Lloyd had been playing cards. "I'll pay," she said, as if she and Rose didn't draw money from the same source. She stepped in front of Rose and grabbed the toaster.

"Mom, that's the toaster," Rose said.

Fiona clutched it. She dug her fingers into the slots and said to the scared delivery man, "What's the damage?"

Over supper Rose and Lloyd did their best to pass the incident off as an understandable mistake: toaster, purse— both white and a certain size, both next to each other on the counter. Fiona said, "Nice try." Her closed expression signaled to Rose that lapses of this nature were more common than she let on. Rose grew apprehensive. She didn't have time for her mother to take a downward turn.

She declined coffee and slipped into the alley for a smoke. The homeless guys, the brothers, weren't there. She watched the clouds. They were like fast-forward movie clouds, rolling and blue gray. She stubbed out her cigarette on a telephone pole and went upstairs to consult the forecasts. Everybody was calling for clear conditions until tomorrow.

She opened her window. From here she could see how localized the clouds were. She wanted to phone Victor, but she had to stop acting so uncharacteristically interested in the forecast. Anyway, he'd be phoning her soon. She stood over her computer and read comments on the website: "Gable holds his binoculars upside down in *The Misfits* and *Soldier of Fortune*." "Speaking of gaffes, has anyone noticed that the stallion in *The Misfits* is a mare?"

When Victor did call, Rose refrained from asking about the weather and asked about his day. He told her that he had steam-cleaned his carpets to kill the dust mites. Dust mites didn't bite you, he said, they were after your dead skin. Under magnification a dust mite looked like an elephant.

There was an eerie green pooling between the clouds. "I think we're in for some rain here," she finally allowed herself to say.

"Yeah, you might see a pop-up."

Her stomach cinched.

"Over here it's all altocumulus." He heard the thunderclap at her end. "There it is."

"I should go see how they're doing downstairs," she said and crossed to the door and turned the lock.

"Guess whose birthday it is tomorrow? I'll give you two hints."

At the best of times she despised this game. "Just tell me."

"He overcame dyslexia."

Rose's vision began to sharpen. "Victor, I've really got to go. Sorry. We'll talk later." She turned the phone off and grabbed a handful of Kleenex.

The preliminaries sped by: the flecks, the fortresses, the nausea, the feeling of her skin cooling and tightening.

Φ

She was in an old, wide-bodied taxi, bumping down a section of chewed-up city street narrowed by construction cones the same orange as the setting sun reflected in office windows up ahead. She had on peach-colored capris and clutched a mauve shoulder bag. Her feet, as always, were cold.

The cab stopped for a red light. It was beginning to rain, and the driver turned on his wipers. "Cha-cha-cha," he said, nodding toward a vacant storefront.

A man wearing a poncho and sombrero stood strumming a guitar. Beside him a Chihuahua in a miniature version of the same outfit danced on its hind legs.

"It's female," said the driver.

So it was. A pair of distended teats poked out from the bottom of the poncho.

"A transvestite dog," said the driver.

The sight upset Harriet, and she looked away. The light changed, the cab lurched forward, and Rose was back in her body.

She had been gone all of two minutes. She went through the ritual of crying and wiping her bloody nose, and then she moved to the sofa and curled up.

Rain pummeled the roof. She thought of her mother saying that when you're pregnant, all you see are babies. All Harriet saw were nursing dogs, first the hound from the redbrick apartment building, and now this cross-dresser. Why was it, Rose wondered, that whenever she entered Harriet, something odd or emotional or coincidental was about to happen? Maybe the episodes needed the prospect of a stimulating event before they could launch. Maybe the phone had to be about to ring, or Marsh had to be about to describe Rose as Rose listened in, or David had to be on his way over with Lesley not far behind. Maybe a man had to be putting a poncho and sombrero on his little dog.

◐

She runs into Ava at the PetSmart on Eglinton Avenue. It seems that she, Rose, owns a cat. Ava is standing on a stepladder and counting litter boxes. "I've been working here for years," she says.

"Nobody told me," Rose sobs. She clings to her sister's ankles.

"Answer the door," Ava says.

"What door?" Rose says and hears the knocking.

She had slept through *Hidalgo* and intermission and the first part of *The Misfits*. She assumed the person outside her office must be Victor.

It was her friend Robin.

"So you *were* sleeping," Robin said. "Fiona thought you would be."

"Hello," Rose said and went toward her.

"Just let me take this off," Robin said. She removed her dripping raincoat, and the two women hugged. Beneath them men yelled, "Six, seven, eight." It was the scene where Marilyn hits the paddle ball.

"This is a nice surprise," Rose said.

Robin limped to the sofa. "You didn't get my messages?"

"What's the matter with your leg?"

"Oh, this new kid, he has major anger overload. He smashed my knee with a metal truck. Elaine wants him out before he kills the babies, but we're his third day care in a year." She sat and took a bottle of juice from her overflowing bag. "Didn't you get my messages?"

Rose glanced at the window. Blue sky, shredded stratus. "What messages?"

"I left one yesterday, and one half an hour ago. I guess you were conked out."

Half an hour ago Rose was inside Harriet. She had a vague recollection of yesterday's message. "Oh, right, you were meeting someone."

"And then coming by for a quick visit. You fast-forward, you miss the important part."

"Sorry," Rose said, "I forgot." She sat down and waved at the general chaos. "I'm swamped. I'm behind in everything."

"Don't worry, I can't stay. The meeting ran late. I just thought I'd pop in."

"No," Rose said. "Stay." Robin was her oldest friend. They'd met in grade seven and were drawn to each other, the two big tall girls, the white one with the tragedy and the black one newly arrived with her adoptive white parents from London, Ontario, where the population was so uniformly Caucasian that when Robin was three and saw a little black child walking down the street, she stopped in her tracks, awestruck, and said, "Look, another Robin."

"It's like we're in a soap opera," she said now. "Have you ever noticed how in soap operas they're always showing up at each other's doors?"

This made Rose smile. She was dying to tell Robin about the episodes, but how could she? Even somebody who believed in God and the angels (and Robin did not) would question her sanity.

"What?" Robin said.

Rose realized she'd been staring. "I've missed you," she said truthfully. Ever since Robin had gotten married and moved to Oshawa, they hardly saw each other. "Have you eaten? Do you want some popcorn?"

"God, no, please. Fiona already offered me a bucket. How's she doing? She seemed a bit confused."

"She's up and down. More up than down."

"She said she hoped Brandon and I were sorting out our troubles."

"Actually, that was sharp of her. I used you as an alibi. I told her we were meeting for a drink to discuss your marriage."

"When really you were . . ."

"Going to this party."

"You can't go to parties?"

"She thinks I'm out all night fooling around on Victor."

Robin raised her eyebrows. She drank her juice. She had never spoken against Victor, but he wasn't her favorite person, Rose knew that. When Robin lived in Toronto and had them for dinner at her apartment, Victor picked at his food and extracted the beans, nuts, carrots, uncooked tomato skins, and whatever else brought on his allergies. Also, he didn't exactly keep it a secret that operating a day-care center was his idea of hell.

Rose glanced again at the window. Inky clouds were rising above the billboard. "Are we in for another storm?" she said. "Is that possible?" She got up and went to her desk.

"You should see our backyard," Robin said. "It's a swamp. What are you doing?"

Rose was Googling *Toronto weather radar*. "I need to check something."

"So you went to a wild party."

"Moderately wild."

"Was Victor there?"

Heavy rainfall warning, Rose read. *Risk of flooding in low-lying areas.*

"No, Victor was *not* there," Robin concluded.

Rose heard thunder. "You know what?" she said. "I'm sorry, but I've got to write this e-mail."

"Yeah, and Brandon's waiting for me. To help sort out our *troubles*." She heaved herself up. "Well, I was in town, so."

"I'll call you soon," Rose said, standing and going over. "We'll get together."

"Oh," Robin said softly.

"What?"

"Everything's . . ." She looked around the room. She raised her hands and moved them here and there.

Rose watched in a state of immobilizing disbelief. It's the office, she thought. The office triggers the episodes. It's me, she thought, I'm spreading them, they're viruses. She had a calamitous image of the entire theater being infected and patrons falling left and right, men entering the minds of young girls. She pictured herself and Robin groping toward each other's consciousness through the illicit dark of Harriet's. All this before Robin, completing her sentence, said, "spinning."

"Spinning?"

Robin drank the rest of her juice. "That's better," she gasped.

"So are you all right?" The thunder was closer now. The scar on Robin's jaw was coming into focus.

"Yeah, I'm okay. It's my new blood-pressure medication."

"Do you feel sick or . . . ?"

"No, it's just these sudden five-second dizzy spells. I've had two today. That one was strong, though. A good thing I don't drive." She put on her raincoat and gave Rose a hug.

"You'd better see your doctor," Rose said. Her vision swarmed with flecks.

"Don't worry, I will. Okay, I'm late. I'm off."

"Be careful on the stairs."

Far across the room, too far, was Rose's desk. Her skin cooled and tightened. She sank onto the carpet.

☯

The lumpy seat cushion under her thighs, the smell of lemon oil and caramel corn, the pillars crowding her peripheral vision, the movie up on the screen—every passing second substantiated Rose's impression that she was beneath the entrance to her office, where, in her own body, she had collapsed. If the office floor gave way, she would fall on top of herself.

A forearm pressed companionably against hers. Marsh's, surely. Rose's impulse was to race down to the auditorium. Except—oh, right—she was inside Harriet. An asphyxiating terror seized her. I'm going to die in here, she thought, but then a blaze of anger from Harriet wrested her attention back to the screen.

Eli Wallach, at the wheel, was chasing down a small herd of mustangs. Marilyn sat in the passenger seat, Gable and Montgomery Clift stood in the flatbed. Wallach pulled up beside a mare who had separated from the herd, and Clift tossed a rope around her neck, whereupon a tire attached to the rope's other end jumped off the truck and dragged her to a halt. Gable laughed and whooped. He loved this. Marilyn hated it. So did Harriet.

So did Rose. She had seen *The Misfits* three times, but not until now did she appreciate that the horses weren't acting. This was real for them: their lungs really burned, their starved bodies really ran themselves out. No wonder her parents hadn't let Ava see it.

Harriet felt nauseous. She got her bag and stood.

"Are you all right?" said the person next to her. Yes, it was Marsh.

"I just need to pee," she said.

As soon as she was out of the auditorium, she headed for the stairs. The runner's hectic flower-and-crown pattern dazzled her, and she almost vomited on the landing. She made it to the top and stood clutching the newel post. Her eyes traveled across the paneling and paused on the unmarked office door behind which Rose sat.

The door was ajar.

Other way, Rose thought. *The washroom's the other way.*

Harriet seemed transfixed by the door's brass-and-porcelain knob. Maybe it interested her. Or maybe this was Rose's mind craving her body. If the door should open. If Rose should see herself *from outside herself.* The instant, traceless, mutual extermination she envisioned seemed inescapable, only seconds away. *Go left*, she begged. *Other way.*

Her hand—Harriet's hand—slipped from the post. She glanced right.

Left. Go left.

She went left.

She locked herself in the first cubicle and let out a breath that couldn't begin to convey Rose's relief. Harriet sat on the toilet seat and cried. Rose felt as if she cried, too, first for the horses and then over a memory of Ava allowing the friendless, brain-damaged boy from across the street to chew the end of her ponytail.

The washroom door thumped open. She flushed the toilet. Last year Rose had installed "control roll" dispensers, and you could tear out only a measly strip at a time. She blew her nose. The door thumped again, not a second woman coming in, the first woman leaving.

At the sink Harriet was drawn to her reflection endlessly multiplied in the mirrors behind her. For Rose the most distant reflections were Ava. She had a peculiar, ghostly feeling of leaning forward through an expansion in the web of Harriet's consciousness. This circumstance, however phantasmal, unbalanced Harriet. She gripped the sink. Seconds passed. The web sealed over, Rose's mind retreated, and Harriet, regaining her balance, picked up her purse and left.

Straight down the stairs she went, over to the concession, where Fiona, inches taller, her freckles and wrinkles distinctly visible, stood watching.

Did Fiona see Ava's eyes? How could she not? Her expression softened, although it would have anyway for a pretty young woman. "That's a smart jacket you're wearing," she said.

Harriet also softened. "Thank you."

Fiona put her glasses on to peer at the jacket's cuff. "It's a cotton-linen blend, isn't it?"

"It might be. I'm not sure."

"Do you mind if I feel?"

"No, not at all."

Fiona rubbed the sleeve between her fingers. "Cotton-linen." She took the glasses off. "That's why it doesn't crease."

From Rose's vantage she and Fiona were looking straight into each other's eyes. Fiona, from her vantage, should have been looking into *Ava's* eyes, both daughters vicariously present to her, and yet she betrayed not the slightest recognition. Rose found this strangely terrible.

"Now what would you like?" Fiona said.

"Do you have Perrier?"

"In the refrigerator there. Help yourself."

The bottle was big in her little hand. Her money she kept in a vintage upholstered change purse. She unfolded a five-dollar bill and held it out to Fiona, who took it and snapped it professionally.

"Horse killers!" Marilyn screamed from the auditorium.

She flinched.

"They set them free," Fiona said. "Although I'm giving away the ending."

Harriet was struggling not to appear as disturbed as she felt. "I don't think I'll go back in." She dropped her change, three quarters and a dime. Fiona scooped it up and put it firmly in her palm. How eerie for Rose, the touch of her mother's dry fingers.

There were voices to one side of them. They glanced over. A man and woman had entered the vestibule and were shaking out their umbrellas.

Fiona, turning back, said with sudden conviction, "I know who you are. You're the youngest Beaton girl."

"No, actually. I'm not."

Jenny Beaton—Rose had gone to high school with her—was dark and short, otherwise nothing like Harriet. Nothing at all like Ava.

"Jenny," Fiona said. "Jenny Beaton."

"I'm Harriet Smith."

"Well, I could have sworn," Fiona said. She nudged the box of straws closer. "Harriet. That's a name you don't hear every day."

"I'm the only one I know."

"It has substance. Are you a lawyer?"

"I'm an editor at a publishing company."

"Which one?"

"Goldfinch Publishers."

"I haven't heard of them."

"Have you heard of Vireo?"

"Why don't you ask *him*?" Fiona said, nodding past her.

She looked and saw Lloyd walking from the projection booth stairs to the ticket stand. When she looked back, Fiona's mouth was knit into a lewd smirk. *She has dementia*, Rose thought, stricken, but Harriet seemed to know. "I just might," she said.

The smirk roamed her way. "What?"

"I just might ask him."

"He's not your husband," Fiona scolded in her Irish accent.

"No, he isn't. I'm single."

Fiona squinted. "All on your own, then, are you?"

Oh, Mom, Rose thought. She could have died for her.

Somebody came out of the auditorium. It was Marsh. "They cut them loose," he said.

"I heard."

"I'm sorry, Harriet. I thought it was about *rescuing* mustangs."

"Well, we had a nice talk." She raised her Perrier to Fiona, and Marsh pivoted, but Fiona stepped away and began industriously scooping popcorn. She was herself again, Rose could tell. She was aware of having suffered a lapse and afraid of what she might have said or done.

"Let's just go," Marsh said quietly.

The rain had ended. The evening smelled of earthworms flooded from their holes. Rose was feeling emotional about her mother. Harriet was feeling defensive. "I've cut down," she said, lighting her cigarette.

He knows she's pregnant, Rose thought.

"Am I saying anything?" Marsh protested.

"You're thinking it loudly enough."

He knows.

"What happened back there?" he said.

"With the mother? We were talking, she was really sharp, really lovely, and then she . . . she went somewhere else."

"I noticed the ticket fellow keeping an eye on her."

"Poor thing. It's Alzheimer's, right?"

Marsh took a long stride over a puddle. "The daughter only said dementia."

"At least she's working, making herself useful."

"In beautiful surroundings."

"Oh, when I went upstairs to the washroom? I had this incredible déjà vu. Everything was familiar. The carpet, the railing. The doorknobs."

"Those massive washroom doorknobs?"

"No, the ones . . ."

Their voices faded behind the commotion in Rose's mind. A real, undeniable leak had sprung between

Harriet and her. What else could account for the déjà vu? But it wasn't déjà vu, it was Rose's lifelong acquaintance with the hallway swelling into the vacuum created by Harriet's ignorance of it. I'm wearing away at her, she thought, and tried to imagine what that might mean.

A painful spasm in her upper back returned her to the present moment. She and Marsh were on a side street. They were crossing to a rusty old Tercel. He unlocked the doors, and they climbed in and lowered their windows.

"Are you sure you don't want to wait until you can lie down?" he said.

"No, because it'll settle in, and then it'll last all night." She reached behind her to touch the sore place. "If we can get it now."

"Come closer."

She shunted over as far as the gearshift.

"Lean into my hands."

She did, and he began to massage his thumb down her scapula. She cringed. Rose, who had her own back problems, knew this type of hurt.

"Breathe," he said.

She blew out air, sucked it in, and he found the knot and worked at it until it loosened and disappeared. "Oh, that's good," she said.

He started massaging her shoulders. Her head dropped. This, now, was pure pleasure, so relaxing that Rose fell into a reverie of lying on a tropical beach. Since she had never been south, she wondered if she wasn't eavesdropping on a memory of Harriet's. There was an end-of-the-world quality to the wind clattering the palm fronds, the waves sloshing far up onto the sand, and over the water a mist that made for an impression of blue light trapped and sparkling between panes of glass.

"Am I forgiven?" he asked after what felt like an entire afternoon.

"For what?"

"The movie."

"No. But that was great, thank you. You have magic hands." She moved to her side of the car. "How are you with abortions?"

"Harriet," he chided.

"I'm joking," she said, stung, and she fished in her bag for her Du Mauriers. He got the car going. "Can we stay a bit longer?" she asked.

He turned the engine off. She held her cigarette out the window. Neither of them spoke. Rain from the trees and power lines hit her arm when the wind gusted. She was looking at the BMW parked in front of them: its license plate, *NUN*.

"So this is what," he said, "day three of the antide-pressants?"

"Day two."

"They take a couple of weeks to kick in, right?"

"One week, I'm hoping." She puffed on her cigarette. "Do nuns drive BMWs?"

"Not as a rule. Not as a *habit*."

She smiled over at him, hunkered and crammed into his tiny, crumbling car, this good man.

"It's a nihilist," he said. "NONE was taken."

Harriet's attention had moved on. "I can't believe how reasonable she was."

"Who are we talking about?"

"Lesley."

"Ah, the wife."

"She was like a social worker, and David and I were these punks she had to straighten out."

"I think you should tell him."

"I'm not telling him."

"He might choose you."

She shook her head. She smiled, but she felt bleak.

"It's really over, then," Marsh said.

She tossed the cigarette. "It's really over."

☉

In the episode's aftermath it dawned on Rose that Harriet and Marsh were parked no more than a few blocks away.

She rushed into the hall. At the top of the stairs she stopped. Where were they *exactly*? She remembered having gone north, crossing an intersection, turning onto a side street. She remembered the BMW. Otherwise, she couldn't summon a single marker.

She would never find them in time.

She grasped the newel post. She cried a little. She went into the ladies' and stroked the door latches and sat on the toilet seat. She hoped to pick up a psychic charge from the things Harriet had touched so recently, but she was far more caught up in the déjà vu, which she took as proof of mind transmission. From now on when she spoke to Harriet, she might really be heard, and to hear an inner voice separate from your own (a disembodied voice if ever there was one) would be like hearing the voice of God.

She left the washroom in a kind of delirium. Midway along the corridor the silence from below finally reached her.

Her mother and Lloyd were at the kitchen table. A sherry bottle stood between them, and they each had a glass.

"Here she is!" Fiona said gaily.

"Mom, what are you doing?" said Rose, for whom comprehension seemed to be clicking through those blurring, sharpening lenses the optometrist slides in front of your eyes. "You can't mix Reminyl with alcohol."

"It seems I can," Fiona said.

"I wasn't thinking," Lloyd said. He went to take Fiona's glass.

But she held it to her chest and said, "I'm fine," as if turning down a refill.

He collected his own drink and the saucer he'd been using as an ashtray and carried them to the counter. A couple of puffs on his cigarette, and he threw it out the open door. Rose picked up the sherry bottle.

"Help yourself," Fiona said.

It was Lloyd's cigarette Rose wanted. "I'm driving," she reminded her mother.

Fiona made a dismissive sound. "Anyway," she said, "Lloyd's been telling me about his cousin. He was a famous mascot for a baseball team. Tell her, Lloyd. Tell her what he would do. Mad Dog McNutt."

Lloyd was closing and locking the alley door. "Another time."

Fiona charged on: "He would throw a Frisbee, chase it down, and catch it himself, in his own mouth." She sipped her drink. "Now that's what I call a go-getter."

She wasn't slurring or incoherent. Rose put the sherry back on the shelf. Her mother would drink when and however much she liked, if not from this bottle, then from one she could easily walk up the street and buy.

"Mad Dog McNutt," Fiona said, raising her glass.

"McNeil," Lloyd said.

"Mad Dog McNeil," Fiona said.

Lloyd glanced at his watch, and it came to Rose that, but for his letting himself be plied with stale sherry on unpaid overtime, her mother would have gone up to the office and found her blacked out. Suddenly abjectly grateful, she offered to drive him to the subway. "You've missed your bus," she said.

"I'll walk. It's high summer out there."

The kitchen light lent his tattoos a metallic glaze, and on his bicep Rose saw the words *Temet Nosce*. Know thyself, she translated, remembering it from somewhere. It seemed like a message to her personally, like a postscript to the episode: get your own head straight before hanging around in someone else's.

He saw her looking and smiled.

"How do you do that?" she said.

"Know yourself? Meditate, for one."

"Meditate," Rose said doubtfully.

"Shut your eyes and look into the nothingness."

Rose shut her eyes and envisioned Harriet's face. She opened them and thought that if she knew herself lately it was only by virtue of knowing she wasn't Harriet.

Fiona stood. "Where did I put my purse, where did I put my purse?" she said with a slur now, and an accent. Either she had suffered one of her ministrokes or the liquor was hitting her. "We're driving you to the subway station," she told Lloyd. "No, no, no." Holding up a hand. "That's how it is."

Once they were in the car, Fiona decided they would drive him all the way home. "I want to see where you live," she said over his objections. Rose hoped it wasn't someplace depressing. She let the two of them do the talking—Fiona laughing and wisecracking—and re-played the episode. The car seemed to steer itself on rails.

Lloyd lived in the basement apartment of a plain brown low-rise across from a Dairy Queen. So not de-pressing, more like poignant, especially since a cat wait-ed in the window.

"My daughter's," he said.

"What's her name?" Fiona asked.

"My daughter or the cat?"

"You've told me your daughter's name. Although, what is it again?"

"Ariel. The cat's Napoleon."

"Better than the other way around!"

After Lloyd got out, Fiona moved to the front seat. Rose, looking at Napoleon, thought she should marry Lloyd and save his daughter and cat from basement apartments. She imagined the sex, Lloyd's weathered face as he labored toward orgasm, and was engulfed by a richly erotic feeling.

Fiona was singing, "Let's all go to the Dairy Queen, the Dairy Queen, the Dairy Queen."

Rose returned to the episode. Harriet joking about having an abortion frightened her. She rewound to Thursday and Harriet saying, "I need to know the option of suicide exists, I don't need to act on it." This Rose understood. She'd had her black moments after Ava's death, she knew that telling yourself *I can always jump off a bridge* conferred a sense of vigilance and security, like carrying a gun in a sketchy neighborhood. Except, why was Harriet talking about suicide in the first place? Her circumstances weren't unspeakably horrible. She had a good job, friends, a devoted sister.

But the sister was worried, and Harriet took antidepressants. She must be thin-skinned, Rose thought.

Ava had been thin-skinned. She had never despaired about her own circumstances, however, so there was that difference. Animals suffering and dying, physical deformities, beautiful fragile beloved objects getting wrecked, this was what had pained Ava, sometimes wilting her to the ground in a type of faint she called "the funny feeling."

"What's the number one suicide profession?" Fiona said in her normal voice.

Rose looked over at her, slumped in her seat. "What are you talking about?" she said. That her mother's mind should be running in the same morbid current was extremely unsettling.

Fiona attempted to sit straight. "The people who commit the most suicides. Lloyd was saying, but I forget. Number two is dentists. Number three is mascots."

"Lloyd's cousin killed himself?"

"Not him. Others."

"How are you doing?"

"Mad Dog McNutt. How am I doing? I'm three sheets to the wind. That's all right."

"It's just with Reminyl, it's dangerous."

"A man is about to be executed," Fiona said, letting herself slump again. "He's lashed to a post. Blindfolded. They offer him a cigarette. He says, 'I'm trying to cut down.'"

Rose was silenced. Then she said, as she was obliged to say, "You might live a long time yet."

Fiona grunted.

AUGUST 1982

It was true about Gordon and the yellow hard hat—it never came off. In the unshaded yard where he taught Ava to ride, sweat rained down his face, but the hat stayed on.

"He would be cooler in a cowboy hat," Rose said to Ava.

"He has to sometimes climb up on roofs," Ava said sternly.

For all the things Ava knew about Gordon, she didn't know he had stepdaughters who fought like a pair of weasels. Apparently Gordon had spoken of them only to Rose, since neither of her parents mentioned them, either. Whenever he ambled over to her during a lesson, she prayed it wasn't to talk about the stepdaughters.

Not until the beginning of August did she let herself believe he had forgotten his plan or changed his mind. "The coast is clear!" she wrote in her diary on August 2.

On August 5 he arrived with the stepdaughters in tow. It was shortly after lunch, a hot day between riding-lesson days. Fiona was washing her paintbrushes in the kitchen sink, and Ava and Rose, in the living room, were working on a Popeye jigsaw puzzle. Ava heard the truck and ran to the window. "It's Gordon, he's stopping!" she cried. Less rapturously, she said, "He's got two girls with him."

While they were still on the porch stairs, Gordon introduced them: Brianna Grace and Shannon. "We happened to be in the neighborhood," he said.

What neighborhood? Rose thought sourly. Her mother said, "Come in, come in! Isn't this a treat!"

Brianna Grace, the younger one, cowered. She wouldn't let go of Gordon's overalls, so the two of them squashed through the door together. She wore a shiny pink party dress trimmed in gold sequins, some of which hung from their threads. Over her shoulder and secured across her belly was a hard leather purse, a lady's purse. Her ears stuck out of her mousy hair. To Rose, she looked like a girl in a movie about poor farm people.

Shannon looked like a tough city girl, lean and boyish, short spiky hair, black sneakers, a black sleeveless

T-shirt that showed off her biceps. She ducked past Gordon and went to the window, where she fell into an examination of her many rings.

"Have you had your lunch?" Fiona asked.

"We're all tanked up, yep," Gordon said.

"What about some nice cold lemonade?"

Gordon put it to the stepdaughters. "Lemonade?"

Shannon responded directly to Fiona, an unsmiling but not unsociable "Sure, thanks." Brianna Grace nodded with her face against Gordon's stomach. It was hard for Rose to associate her with the word *weasel*, let alone imagine her fighting like one.

"So, Rosie," Gordon said, "I was telling Shannon how I thought you was thirteen, the same as her."

Rose hugged herself to conceal her breasts. They had started growing in June, along with the vegetable garden and at the same terrible speed.

"Rose is eleven," said Ava in a bright, instructing voice.

"And you, Red, if I'm not mistaken, have a tenth birthday coming up."

Ava's face opened. "On August thirty-first."

"Brianna Grace is ten this November." He rubbed his hands as though, with their ages established, they should start playing a game.

"I didn't know you had stepdaughters," Ava said shyly.

"Sure you did." He jiggled his hard hat. "Ah, cripes," he muttered, and Brianna Grace released him and put her thumb in her mouth.

"Why don't we all move to the table?" Fiona said, lifting the tray of drinks.

Gordon unbuckled his chin strap.

"Here comes the dent," Shannon quietly singsonged.

He tore the hard hat off.

Ava let out a cry. Rose froze. Above his right ear was a purple, scooped-out place, a less drastic but still grisly version of Rose's story about him missing the top of his skull.

He ground his palm in it. The dent. "Sorry for the freak show," he said. "It's where I had the tumor removed."

Fiona put down the tray. "Tumor?"

"You didn't hear?" He scratched his bald head all over. "This trial drug makes you feel like a thousand black flies are going at you." He pulled out a chair, and Brianna Grace climbed into the one next to him. "Yeah," he said, "so February seven I had a malignant tumor removed. Size of a golf ball. I thought you would've heard."

"We had no idea. I'm so sorry. Would cortisone cream help?"

"Nah, creams are useless."

Ava weaved unsteadily to the table. "Give her a glass," Fiona told Rose, but then she came over herself and cupped Ava's hands around a glass and said, "Drink."

"I'm okay," Ava murmured.

"I wasn't going to go public until I got the all-clear," Gordon said. He put his hard hat back on. "Everyone found out anyways, from the nurses or whatever." His eyes followed Shannon as she walked past the empty chair beside him and sat next to Ava. "Brain cancer. I'm going to beat it, no question about that."

"Of course you are," Fiona said heartily. She had opened a box of Oreos and was dumping them onto a plate. "A positive attitude is half the battle."

"I'm back to my fighting weight. The cut is healing up." He held out his arm.

"I can barely see it," Ava submitted tremulously.

"Yep, it's healing up good."

To make room for the cookies, Fiona pushed aside the center tray with its paraphernalia of salt and pepper shakers, Bicycle playing cards, hand lotion, sugar packets, and a ceramic cow. Shannon reached for the cards, poured them from the box, and began a loose, overhand shuffle. She had a ring on every finger and on both thumbs, smooth rings like metal nuts but brown and grained like wood.

"Oreos," said Gordon and helped himself to one and gobbled it down. They all took one then. Brianna Grace slipped hers into her purse. Shannon pulled hers apart and licked the icing with a private, pleasured expression Rose found shocking. Also shocking was that Brianna Grace put another cookie in her purse, and then another and another. She was emptying the plate.

Nobody else noticed or cared. Gordon and Fiona were discussing his wife's job at the Honda plant, her shift change from nights to days. "Which is why I'm dragging the girls around," he said. He turned back to Brianna Grace. "Isn't that right, Bree?"

Brianna Grace snapped the purse shut.

"We can't leave 'em on their own," he said, "or they're at each other's throats."

He wants to leave them here, Rose realized, alarmed.

Fiona said, "Well, at least you're spending time together, the three of you. You see more dads with their kids nowadays."

"He's not our dad," Shannon said.

"Anyways," Gordon said. He pushed himself up. Brianna Grace stood as well, making no effort to conceal her bulging purse.

"I better be off," Gordon said.

"But you only just got here," Fiona said.

"I'm getting a blood test."

"Sit down," Shannon told her sister. "We're staying."

"Oh, you are?" said Fiona, catching on at last. "Well, you're most welcome."

"That'd help me out a lot," Gordon said.

"I was afraid you were all going to disappear!"

"I shouldn't be more'n a couple of hours." He began edging toward the door, hands high. Brianna Grace clamped onto his leg. He warned her with several clipped *Hey*s but she clung like a drowning person. "She pulls this at the clinic," he told Fiona, who crouched to Brianna Grace's level and asked did she want to see the pony?

"She's afraid of ponies," Shannon said.

"Okay, that's enough," Gordon said. He roughly yanked the child by her wrists. She screamed, and there was the gap where Shannon had knocked out her tooth with a pool cue.

"Do you want to see my dolls?" cried Ava. Ava, who hated having her dolls touched.

Brianna Grace let Gordon go. "Are they Barbies?" she lisped.

"I have seven Barbies," Ava said.

Gordon made his escape. The little girls went upstairs. "Mind the paint tray!" Fiona called after them. To

Rose and Shannon she said, "Can I leave you to entertain yourselves?"

No! Rose thought.

"Sure," Shannon said. "There's lots to do here." She reached again for the playing cards.

"If you want to run through the sprinkler, Rose will lend you a bathing suit."

When she was gone, Shannon said, "I'm not the running-through-sprinklers type." She resumed her casual shuffling. "Have you ever heard of ring power?" she asked.

Rose said she hadn't.

"Okay," Shannon said. "The power of the universe comes to the earth through plant life. So if you wear wood on your fingers, but even if you wear vines or stems, you grow stronger in the five ways each of your fingers stands for." She put down the cards. "Honesty," she said, holding up her thumb. She tapped each of her other fingers in turn: "Health, creativity, judgment, memory. Can you remember that?"

"I think so," Rose said.

"Honesty, health, creativity, judgment, memory," Shannon said. "You have interesting hands."

"I do?" Rose opened them. She turned them over.

"*Very* interesting," Shannon said. She stood and began to walk around, plucking at her hair, spiking it out. "There are seven types of hands. Your hands are a mixture of two types, the thinking type and the practicality type." She nudged her foot at the curled linoleum under which the ants, long since vanished, had carried crumbs. "Dry rot," she pronounced. She opened the cutlery drawer, took out the spatula, and slapped it hard on the counter.

Rose grew uneasy. "Do you want to play cards?"

"Like what?"

"Rummy?"

"I always win for two reasons. One, I have an IQ of a hundred and forty-five. That's genius level."

Rose didn't doubt it.

"Two, I have the third eye. I see pictures in my mind. When I play cards, I see what's in the other person's hand ninety percent of the time."

It seemed impossible to question this. "But that's not every time," Rose pointed out.

Shannon dropped the spatula back in the drawer. "It's your funeral."

She won game after game. She would shut her eyes for a few seconds, and then discard something Rose had no use for. Between these silent moments she talked about magnets and magnetic attraction. Magnetic people didn't need people, and that was what made them attractive. The opposite of magnetic was repulsive. Repulsive people needed people. "Brianna Grace is a perfect example of repulsive," she said. "Obviously." A perfect example of magnetic was Shannon's boyfriend. The two of them played strip poker. "He's down to, like, a sock," she said, "and I've still got all my clothes on. It's a riot."

Rose's face burned.

"Have you ever played strip poker?"

"No," Rose said, tortured. She discarded without thinking: a five of diamonds.

"I'll take that," Shannon said. "Well, if you ever do"—she laid down her hand, winning yet again—"your glasses count as clothes. Rings don't count, glasses do." She stood and went to the dining room doorway. "This is a solid house. You can't hear anybody. In my house the walls are some kind of crappy Sheetrock that leaks toxic gas. It's giving Brianna Grace brain damage. But try telling that to Gordon. He has no clue about toxic gas. He's so uneducated."

"But he thinks he's so smart," Rose said. Here at last was a subject she could contribute to.

"He doesn't own a single book. I've never seen him read even the newspaper."

"His grammar is bad," Rose said.

Shannon crossed to the back window, which had a view of Major Tom under his shelter. "That is one well-hung pony," she said.

"What?" Rose said, and then she understood and covered her mouth and said, "I know!"

Shannon pointed to the fruit bowl. "Can we have that banana?"

They went out to the paddock, and Shannon straddled the top rail. "People think ponies and horses only like apples, but they like bananas better," she said. "Come on, boy," she said, wagging the banana. Major Tom moseyed over. He tugged the banana out of its skin and chewed as he chewed everything: thoroughly and rhythmically, his mouth making the clopping sound of hooves on pavement. "Good boy," Shannon said. "Hungry boy." She hurled the skin toward the manure pile. "Is that your property?" she asked. "That bush?" She was looking at the woods beyond the cornfield.

"It belongs to the farm on the other concession," Rose said.

Shannon jumped to the ground. "Let's check it out."

"I'm not allowed in the corn, only the first row," Rose said. The restriction shamed her. "My parents are afraid Ava and I will get lost."

"One," Shannon said, "I've been in a hundred cornfields. Two, my third eye sees for ten miles."

The corn was higher than it appeared from outside. "Twelve feet," Shannon judged. Above them the stalks rattled. Down where they were it was windless and humid, prickly when they changed rows, which they kept doing, angling right, correcting a mistake, Rose worried, but Shannon strode confidently—she had a bowlegged cowboy walk, reassuring in itself—and soon the corn thinned, and they climbed a split-rail fence and entered the woods. Rose patted the wrinkled gray bark of the bulky tree nearest her. "It's like an elephant leg," she said.

"It's a beech," Shannon said. "This is an old beech and sugar maple bush. Nobody uses it. Look at all the branches lying everywhere. You could heat a house for an entire winter with what's right here in front of us."

They kept walking. The farther they went in, the cooler it got. Shannon picked up a stick and pointed at plants, naming them. A pretty, pale mushroom like a dollhouse lamp was called destroying angel and was one of the deadliest poisons known to mankind. "It tastes like radishes," Shannon said. "Put some in your enemy's salad, and twelve hours later he's a corpse."

"How do you know all this stuff?" Rose asked. She was greatly impressed. She had never met a genius before.

"Mostly?" Shannon said. She whacked a tree with her stick. "From my dad. He's a commercial fisherman. He had the third eye, but the government destroyed it. You know how? Pumping mind-control chemicals into his well."

They came to an open area bordered on one side by a collapsing rock wall. "This is a good place to build a lean-to," Shannon said and started clearing the ground of stones and twigs. Rose joined in enthusiastically, glad to be useful. They collected long branches, stomped off the unusable parts, and leaned the straight parts against the rocks. Between the branches they stuffed leaves and ferns. The ferns broke from their stems with clean snaps, like celery. "The Indians built lean-tos for shelter on their hunting trips," Shannon said. "The tribe that lived right here, where we are, was the Oneida. People think it was the Ojibwa, but it was the Oneida."

They crawled in and lay on their backs with their knees bent. Shannon opened her hands to the sprays of light—they hadn't filled in every gap after all—and admired her rings. "I should lend you my book on ring power," she said. "If you're a reader, that is."

"I am," Rose said. It hadn't occurred to her that Shannon would want anything to do with her outside of their forced arrangement. "I have lots of books. I have one on the power of the stars and constellations."

Shannon squirmed her arm down between their bodies and got hold of Rose's hand. "Shut your eyes. I'm going to see if we can have a spirit vision together. Are your eyes shut?"

"Yes," Rose said.

Shannon spoke in a tone of incantation: "It's the year 1786. We're Oneida Indian sisters on a hunting trip. We're the only females. We sleep with our knives because you never know about certain sex-crazed warriors."

Rose flinched.

"Don't move," Shannon said. "We do the cooking. We gut fish and scrape hides. We keep the fire going. We never let the fire go out. We pick blueberries and edible plants."

This was better. Rose could see this. She was an Oneida Indian girl. A sensation like a cool mist tingled her skin.

"We make wampum with porcupine quills and with the sinews and the claws of bears."

Her voice was lost to the clamor of singing women, a kind of yelling-singing. Rose couldn't understand the words. She stood barefoot on a smooth rock across from a naked baby girl who lay propped up in a crib. The bottom of the crib was wrapped in white fur. Smoky planks of light fell between the trees. Dogs barked. An old man danced in a tight circle and stabbed his spear at the air. The baby gurgled. Her bristly hair seemed to be on fire, but that was an effect of the sun.

"I need my medicine bag," Shannon said in her regular voice.

Rose returned to herself. "What?"

"I wasn't seeing anything," Shannon said and let go of Rose's hand.

"I was," Rose said. She described the baby and the singing women, the old man.

Shannon scratched her neck. "That isn't what I was saying. I was saying we were in a canoe."

"I was in a woods. Not this one. The trees were taller. The sun was setting."

"Interesting."

"Was it a spirit vision?"

"It sounds like it. I didn't think you had enough power in you to go off on your own, though. Interesting."

"How long did it last for?"

"Ten minutes."

"Really? What time is it?"

They ran back. But their arrival scarcely registered next to the disaster under way—Ava crying on the rag rug, her antique doll, Olga, decapitated, the pieces that had been her china head strewn on the counter. "It broke," was Fiona's explanation. She and Gordon were trying to match the pieces together.

"Brianna Grace kicked her," Ava wept.

The accused sat at the kitchen table nibbling one of the Oreos she had stuffed in her purse. Shannon went over. "Did you kick her doll?" she said.

Brianna Grace nodded. Shannon slapped her.

"Hey!" Gordon yelled.

Brianna Grace lifted her purse over her head and put it on the table. Her cheek was pink from the slap. She stood, tucked a strand of hair behind her ear, and kicked Shannon in the shin.

"Like *that*!" Ava cried.

Another slap.

"Girls, stop it!" Fiona yelled.

Brianna Grace flew into a clawing, punching fury.

"Keep pressing there," Gordon directed Fiona, and like a man shoving onto a crowded subway, he pushed himself between the combatants. Shannon went to the window. Brianna Grace climbed back in her chair and fingered a cookie from her purse. Gordon rejoined Fiona. "Apologies for the interruption," he said.

It was the type of incident that would have sunk Ava to the floor had she not already been there. It stopped her crying, at least. Rose sat next to her and jiggled her foot. Shannon left the kitchen and could be heard opening the French doors to the living room.

Rose found her doing the jigsaw puzzle. "Do you like jigsaw puzzles?" she asked.

"Not really," Shannon said. She frowned at the scattered pieces, and after a moment Rose knelt across from her and continued work on Popeye's spinach can. She thought Shannon might be embarrassed by Brianna Grace, or maybe she was still angry. Rose thought it was nice of Shannon to have come to Ava's defense, but the fight—the abrupt start and stop as much as the silent ferocity—left her feeling estranged.

When the dining room clock struck five, Shannon groaned, "What's taking them so long?" and got up. Rose followed her to the kitchen. Fiona and Gordon were using masking tape to hold the glued pieces together. Olga looked like a burn victim. "You wait, she'll be good as new," Gordon promised a stupefied Ava.

He put Olga in a plastic shopping bag, and he and the stepdaughters left, the plan being for him to paint the doll in his workshop.

On the next riding-lesson day he brought Olga back. The lines in the crimped brown china that represented hair were hidden, but the lines on her face were visible and therefore, if you were Ava, worse than shattered. She traced them with her finger.

"Are you happy, Red?"

Ava nodded.

Nobody asked where he had left the stepdaughters. They weren't welcome. Fiona had tried talking Ava into giving Brianna Grace a second chance, but the prospect of her returning was dreadful to Ava, and Rose had taken Ava's side. The fight had shaken her, and she hoped never to see either girl again.

And yet on the morning of Olga's return she found herself wishing Shannon had come, and after the lesson she walked Gordon to his truck and told him about Shannon offering to lend her a book.

"If she gives it to me, I'll bring it by," he said.

"Or I could get it from your place. My dad could drive me."

"How about I have her call you?" He started the engine.

There was no call that day or the next. The third day, another riding-lesson day, Rose said to Gordon, "I guess Shannon's busy."

"She hasn't called?" he said. "Well, that's Shannon for you. Why don't *you* call?"

Because now that Shannon knew Rose wanted her to call, Rose had to wait. Unless Ava backed down, and then her mother and Shannon's mother could make the arrangements and leave Rose out of it.

She tried bribing Ava with a charm bracelet Ava had always coveted. The charms were different breeds of dog, the eyes colored stones. When that didn't work she appealed to her sister's tender heart: "Brianna Grace doesn't have any friends. We're her only friends."

"What if she throws the china plates?" Ava said. She was reorganizing her shelves to fill the space left by Olga, banished to the underwear drawer.

"Mom won't let her do that."

"She'll do it all of a sudden."

"We'll put the plates away."

"What if she kicks *you*? She almost kicked me!"

"No, she didn't. When?"

"When she was here!" Ava swung her leg around jerkily. "She was going like this! Like this!"

"Okay," Rose said. "Calm down."

She developed an aversion to Ava's sensitivities, a disgust. She couldn't play with her. She said that she wanted to concentrate on her art, and she drew sketches of the barn and the vegetable garden and, secretly, from memory, of Shannon. When normally she would be monitoring the riding lessons, she walked into the cornfield but always got lost and emerged, sweating and hyperventilating, either on the highway or at the edge of the neighbor's mustard property. She lay in the meadow behind the barn and said, "It's the year 1786. I'm an Oneida Indian girl. I sleep with my knife." But without Shannon lying next to her, holding her hand, she was a white girl in the year 1982, and the knife was a stick.

SUNDAY, JULY 3, 2005

After Ava died, Rose very seldom remembered her nighttime dreams. For her, sleep at night was a blank, a kind of death. Since the onset of the episodes, however, she'd been having dreams that carried right into her first waking minutes. This morning's dream was that the brothers knew about her spirit vision, and the brother who was Iroquois said, "White people like being reincarnated Indians, that way they can take our culture and our lands and not feel bad."

Rose woke up protesting. "The girl wasn't *me*," she said out loud. "I couldn't speak the language."

She never thought about the vision or Shannon, or anything having to do with the farm, not if she could help it. But the dream brought the vision to her with an animation and clarity she couldn't avoid—the singing women and dancing man, the naked baby, that entire coherent world belonging to someone else—and she wondered if her brain hadn't resurrected it because it was like an episode. She wondered if, in fact, it hadn't *been* an episode, an inaugural flare-up sparked by something other than thunder and lightning, some force (Shannon's third eye?) strong enough to dispense with the preliminaries and send her back through time.

Had she really believed in Shannon's third eye, though? She couldn't remember, but Shannon's belief might have been enough. She allowed herself to dwell on Shannon, to remember her rings and magnetic-repulsion theory, and even to imagine her as a mother with a bunch of smart, hooligan kids. The last time Rose saw her was at Ava's funeral in the company of the woman from Bert's grocery store. Brianna Grace she spotted in the late nineties pitching foldable colanders on TV, all stylish and lively, recognizable only after the cohost said her name.

Rose peered at her clock radio. A quarter past ten. She found 680 News, climbed out of bed, and opened the drapes. Fluffy cumulus clouds sat on the horizon.

She checked her phone messages. There were four from Victor. The first—"Why aren't you answering?"—made her feel hounded, and she sped through the rest. "Me again—" "I tried the landline—" "Unless you've been abducted, or you've—"

"Married Lloyd," she said, amazed by how completely she'd infiltrated that fantasy after dropping Lloyd off at his apartment. She'd been preparing for bed when she'd finally thought of Victor and their nightly chats. She'd had trouble envisioning his face, and this had seemed like a good enough reason not to call him until the morning. Now that it *was* morning, she still couldn't quite arrange his features into a person she recognized.

The radio meteorologist was issuing a storm warning for between two and three o'clock. Well, Rose had already planned to leave the house earlier than she normally did on Sunday afternoons, since having an episode at home, with Fiona there, was out of the question. An episode at home or any place other than the theater office might not even be possible, but she wasn't willing to test that theory and risk nothing happening.

Windows—standing at them, opening them—she now associated with cigarettes, and she mentally tracked her Du Mauriers to her briefcase on the kitchen counter. If you'd told her a week ago that she, a fanatical nonsmoker, would crave cigarettes . . . How about if you'd told her she would become obsessively protective of a stranger's fetus? She gazed at the disk of ground in the middle of the lawn where neither grass nor weeds grew and attempted to draw from that little crop circle a moral direction. All she came up with was an excuse, an apologetic, you put a barren woman in the body of a pregnant woman and she's bound to feel something.

What she felt at the moment was concern over Harriet's state of mind. *You're okay, you're okay,* she said over and over, pushing the words against the limits of her skull until she had at least convinced herself.

It was one of Fiona's clear mornings. She had showered and dressed and eaten her cereal. At present, in full view of Charles across the road, she was sweeping the front porch of the leaves and twigs brought down by the storms.

"You should have a vicious hangover," Rose told her.

"I never get hangovers," Fiona said.

"You never drink."

"I drank in my day. I had to keep up with your father." She turned her back to the road and started sweeping the top stair. "Your father couldn't hold his liquor, not like I could. I could walk a straight line with a full glass on my head. I won a contest at the Galway."

Rose's father had been notorious for holding his liquor, and while the Galway was a nice touch, Rose didn't doubt that the story was a delusion in line with other recent delusions where Fiona bragged of never-before-mentioned talents. "I'd have loved to see you," she said.

"I won a silver dollar," Fiona said. She lengthened her back and neck, demonstrating her contest-winning form. Or perhaps this display was for the benefit of Charles.

She had made coffee, but Rose's stomach was unsettled, and she filled her mug with Pellegrino and took it and her cigarettes to the den. She opened the window and smoked, watching the sky. After three or four puffs she extinguished the cigarette on the outside wall and sat at her desk and Googled *weather network*. Its forecast was the same as 680's.

She Googled *spirit visions* and read that they were more ecstatic and supernatural, more religious, than the feeling of being an Oneida Indian girl among natural, authentic surroundings. She tried to remember if she'd felt as though she was *inside* the girl. Not really, she concluded. She might have had another experience altogether, something between a spirit vision and an episode. She liked the idea of a precedent, a psychic lineage, but it was also possible that she'd just fallen asleep.

She Googled *baby in the womb*. Up came a full-screen photograph of a fetus at eight weeks. She clicked on "Nine weeks." The fetus had earlobes, fingers, shoulders. At ten weeks the vital organs were fully formed.

You can know too much, she told herself. Magnify a dust mite and you get an elephant. She leaned back in her chair, exhausted. Always exhausted, always queasy. She prodded her belly. It had never been what you would call flat, but now it seemed bloated. Did she have a sympathetic pregnancy? How pathetic that would be! How competitive and self-absorbed!

She went over to the sofa and lay down. Victor called as she was drifting off.

"I got your messages," she said. "My cell was turned off, and I didn't realize until I was home, and then it was late." A dog barked at his end. "Are you outside?"

"I'm near your house."

That woke her. "Where?"

"Davisville and Cleveland."

"What are you doing there?"

"Do you want to go for a walk?" he said aggressively. "Let's go for a walk."

He sounded drunk. Except he never got drunk. "Victor, I should have phoned last night," she said. "I'm sorry."

"I need to see you. I'm not up to faking pleasantries with Fiona. I'll wait here."

"Okay. Give me five minutes."

He was standing at the bus stop and writing in his notebook, getting down some important thought. He wore very blue blue jeans and his loud Hawaiian shirt, tucked in. Normally, her heart opened to see his diligent, unfashionable person in the distance, but the writing had her envisioning all the drafts of his books mounted on his office floor, like foundation pillars for a house you doubted would ever get built, and it came to her that in his perfectionism and terror of being judged, he was like Marlin Lau.

He didn't glance up until she was right next to him. He capped the pen, clipped it to his shirt pocket, and tucked the notebook inside. "Thank you for coming," he said. No kiss, no smile. He looked north and south, then north again, his attention snagged by a basketball net in a driveway. He would never live near such a place, basketball nets equaling children, equaling noise.

"Where should we go?" she asked.

"It doesn't matter," he said and started walking up Cleveland.

She fell in beside him. After so much rain, the lawns were brilliant green, but the roses drooped in the humid warmth. "Let's cross the street," she said.

Even over there, out of the sun, she was hot. Her legs were tired, and she asked him to slow down.

"Sorry," he said.

They walked on. "Are you going to tell me what this is about?" she said.

"In bed Friday, you were different."

"So were you."

"Because you were."

So much for renewing their sex life. "You seemed to enjoy yourself."

A young girl on a bike wobbled toward them, and they stepped off the sidewalk and let her pass. "Bikes are illegal on sidewalks," he said.

"Yeah, kids should ride on the road and get run over."

Another long silence. Then, "Rose, when I say I love you, you don't say it back."

"I do," she said uncertainly.

"You don't. Not since Fiona's diagnosis."

Anger rustled through her. "What's that supposed to mean?"

"It's taken a lot out of you, understandably. And it's only going to get worse."

"So I should pack her off to a nursing home?"

"You should be researching them, yes."

"Don't tell me what I should do with my mother." Now she was the one walking fast. "I know what you think of mothers."

"What are you talking about? I worshiped my mother."

"I'm giving you all the time I can."

He halted. "Rose."

She turned.

"Are you seeing someone?"

"No."

He came over to her and stared into her eyes with his one good eye. He was checking, she knew, for the dilated pupils of a liar.

"I'm not seeing anyone," she said. She wasn't, not in the way he meant, but she didn't trust her pupils to make such fine distinctions, so she dropped her gaze. An earthworm writhed at her feet. In honor of Ava, she picked it up and carried it to the lawn.

"It's my fault, too," Victor said. "We've both grown complacent."

She surprised herself by saying, "We've grown apart."

"Is that what you think?"

She looked at him. "Yes."

"All of a sudden we've grown apart."

"Not all of a sudden." Having no idea what she was going to come out with until she came out with it was like being in Harriet.

"So you're saying we've been growing apart for some time."

His hair was shorter. He must have had it cut yesterday. "For a while," she said gently. "A year."

"A year."

"Or so."

"We've been growing apart for a year. Or so. That's what you think."

"Victor, you know what I think? To be honest? I think we need a break." It wasn't, after all, like being in Harriet, it was like having somebody in *her*, a strong, pragmatic mind that had ordered her to stand back and make way. "A trial separation," she said, emphasizing, as apparently David had not, the word *trial*.

There were more stranded worms. Worms everywhere. She began picking them up and tossing them to safe ground.

"For how long?" Victor said. The fight had left his voice. "A month?"

"That would take us to . . ." He got out his notebook and flipped the pages. "August third."

"Okay." She studied the fat worm in her hand. It might have been a beaded necklace, its pale, swollen middle segment an opal. "How do you tell a male from a female?" she asked.

"Worms are hermaphrodites." He flipped another page. "How should we do this? I call you, or . . ."

"You call."

"What time?"

"Noon?"

"Twelve PM, phone Rose," he said, writing.

She went over to someone's garden and dug a hole and put the worm inside. "Okay," she said. Victor wouldn't want to touch her with all the slime and dirt on her hands. "Until then."

He pocketed the notebook and gave her a tight smile. She hoped her smile wasn't too pitying. Or too buoyant.

She entered the house by the back door, returned to the den, and lay on the sofa. When she woke, the TV was blaring in the living room, and dark clouds were rising above the houses behind theirs. She quickly showered and dressed.

"I'm taking the car," she told her mother. There was a growl of thunder, but she judged it to be some distance away.

Fiona turned the TV down. "That was a long nap."

"I must have got your hangover."

"Try not to get my brain damage."

"What time will you be leaving?"

"The usual time."

"Will you let me pick you up if it's raining?" The episode would be over by then.

"It'll be over by then," Fiona said.

Rose blinked. "What will?"

"The rain. I'll walk."

The storm was moving quickly. Rose rolled through stop signs to beat it, but as she turned onto Mount Pleasant a lightning strike focused her vision. The thunder was a single loud report followed by a horde of flecks already starting to assemble.

She pulled over. You don't have to be in the office was her final thought before exiting her body.

⦶

She stood on a grassy bank above Lake Ontario. The water was slate gray and choppy, giant waves crashing on the industrial rubble that held the bank in place. Near Scarborough Bluffs, windsurfers were still out. To the west, the CN Tower shone against thunderheads branched with flares of light, and glittering inside. Slanted lines below the clouds indicated rain.

She was smoking. She wore blue-striped shorts and red plastic sandals. On the middle finger of her right hand was a ruby ring too big for her. Every time she exhaled, she slid the ruby back into place.

Rose knew where she was: Ashbridge's Bay Park. One Sunday last summer she and Victor had walked along this ridge and argued about the city's decision to fortify the bank with concrete slabs from wrecked sidewalks and building foundations. She'd said they should have used rocks and boulders. Victor had been all for the recycled waste. "It's a money saver," he'd said.

"It's ugly," she said.

"It's efficient," he said.

Inside Harriet now, Rose was staring at the black horizon line. *You could get struck by lightning up here*, she warned. She felt heard but disregarded. She pitched the cigarette, and the ring flew off and slid to the shore.

She looked at it nestled between two stones, the only scrap of color. Harriet seemed not to care.

But she went after it.

Crevices jammed with fine gravel zigzagged down the bank. She followed these paths, clutching the rough edges of slabs. At the bottom, she retrieved the ring, numbly considered it, and put it on her finger. She stepped out of her sandals. She walked into the frigid water and kept walking. Waves smacked the length of her body.

By now Rose understood what was happening, and she was screaming into Harriet's enthrallment. Not until she went under did it come to her that she, too, would die. There was a sound like an electrical short, and then deafness, and then, without Harriet, on her own, she was a million miles above Earth, orbiting sooty smudges and silver shafts that found shape and became demons and angels, hideously elastic demons pissing into rusty tin cans, slender stone angels extending glass goblets.

She accepted a goblet. She brought it to her lips. Immediately, she was back in Harriet and bursting from the water, gulping air, floundering. *It's okay!* Rose said to her. *Calm down!*

She sagged.

Walk!

She let the waves throw her. She stubbed her toe. The pain was sharp, but she didn't react.

She reached the shore, and Rose said, *Put on your sandals.* She put them on. Rose said where to climb, where to step.

At the top she sank to her knees. A warm, steady rain had begun to fall. She lay down. Her heart boomed. Her mouth opened and closed out of sync with her short, labored breaths. She felt for the ruby ring, but it had come off in the water. She felt for her jacket—no, it was a shoulder bag, the mauve one—and tucked it under her stomach.

①

The drive was a feverish twenty minutes of lights turning green at her approach and downpours lasting the space of an intersection. *Stay where you are*, Rose prayed. *Wait for me.*

The shoulder bag absorbed her. If you wanted to drown yourself, why bring a purse that size? For the cigarettes? Why not just bring the cigarettes and lighter, and leave the purse behind? Harriet might have driven to the lake contemplating suicide, but Rose was convinced that she attempted it on impulse. And then shielding the purse from the rain, caring about it, surely this demonstrated a will to live.

She made a right onto the Ashbridge's Bay entry road and slowed down to peer at oncoming drivers. She cruised through the lot, looking for Harriet in parked vehicles before pulling in as close to the water as she could. The sun had come out, and people were strolling on the paths. Rose made a beeline across the spongy lawn. She scanned left and right, dismissing everybody except for a little brunette woman who (Rose detoured for a closer inspection) turned out to be a boy.

The bank lay hidden behind dogwood bushes. Rose was there before she saw that Harriet wasn't. She went to the exact spot, the flattened grass, and looked over the cliff edge. Nothing, no red sandals, no body floating on the jagged water.

She returned to her car, breathing hard now. If she had been found slumped over her steering wheel at the side of the road, the cause of death would have been ruled what? Heart failure? Stroke? In the obituaries on the same day there would be an entry for another woman, this one drowned while swimming alone. Or they might omit the circumstances and just say "suddenly."

At the theater the first thing she did was check that the Weather Network was still calling for clear skies overnight. She then lit a cigarette and read e-mails, dozens and dozens. She hoped Victor had managed to bury himself in work. The truth was, having him out of her life was like having a piano lifted off her chest.

She craved sleep, but she avoided the sofa, and started writing up last night's episode. Lloyd arrived. Lloyd, she thought, jolted, and crept over to the door and shut it.

For tonight's first feature, *The Seven Year Itch*, her father used to get his friend Mr. Donnelly to man the projection booth so that he could sit in the auditorium. This was because on September 15, 1954, her father happened to be visiting New York City, and when he heard that they were filming Marilyn Monroe on Lexington, he ran from West Eighth, a distance of three miles. Near the back of the crowd, nobody taller to block his view, he watched take after take of Marilyn's skirt flying up. "It's not a thing you forget," he would say the rest of his life, as people say of the pyramids.

This evening, at dinner, Fiona asked Rose if she planned to carry on the tradition.

"I don't know," Rose said. It would be the first screening of *The Seven Year Itch* since her father died.

"You can just as easily nap in there as you can in the office," Fiona said. To Lloyd she said, "Rose had a three-hour nap this afternoon. She's tired from being up all night gallivanting."

"From being up all night playing online poker," Rose said, afraid that Fiona would go on to tell Lloyd she was having an affair.

"What?" Fiona said. "Poker?"

"The high-stakes games."

Lloyd passed her a swift, measuring look. "How high?"

"Hundreds of thousands," Rose said, and he smiled into his coffee.

"Oh, you're pulling our leg," Fiona said. "Well, as long as you're not having online sex."

"Mom," Rose groaned. She stood and rinsed her plate.

"I wouldn't even know how to *find* online sex," Fiona said.

Rose felt her face heating up. Her mother was sensing her heightened sexual arousal but, thank God, had yet to zero in on its target. The arousal itself Rose could explain only by thinking she must have brought it back from Harriet, although why it should land on Lloyd and not on one of the younger patrons—or on Victor—left her at a loss.

⊕

She put on a suit jacket (Fiona liked her to dress more formally when she worked in the lobby) and helped at the concession. Also to please her mother, she slipped into the auditorium. She'd seen *The Seven Year Itch* twice and expected to fall asleep.

The opposite happened: she got caught up. Tom Ewell was like her, swinging between one reality and another, entranced by his fluorescent imagination, letting things get out of hand. It was difficult to sit through, but so as not to deal with her clairvoyant mother she stayed until the credits.

She helped at the snack bar again, and then she went to her office for a cigarette. She leaned out the window.

LITTLE SISTER

Her smoke ribboned up to a royal-blue sky. People at the café crossed their legs and drank from their glasses, and welded cell phones to their ears. Eventually the unassailable integrity of the scene reassured Rose.

But her apprehension didn't go away, it transferred to Harriet. Had Harriet told Marsh about her suicide attempt? Rose's feeling was no, she hadn't. The Harriet who had tucked her purse under her stomach had tucked her emotions into such a tight pellet that Rose couldn't see her telling anybody anything. She turned on her computer and found the yoga center's number. "Harriet almost killed herself this afternoon," she would say to Marsh, nothing more. She would use her cell with its blocked number. She would disguise her voice.

The machine answered. She hung up and searched on the website for a list of instructors. Marsh might have gone home, but she needed his last name to find the number.

There was no such list.

Her alibi was that she was meeting some university friends for a drink. "Impromptu girls' night out," she said, avoiding her mother's level look.

She made an effort as she drove to picture Harriet among friends. But it was Ava's drawn, freckled face that accompanied her. She didn't talk to it. Talking to Ava was a comfort she'd never felt entitled to, other than to say, "I'm sorry," and "It should have been me." Flares of guilt and agony in that vein. No matter what Rose said, she had her life.

Although sometimes she had the impression that it wasn't the life she'd started out on. Not lately, not since the onset of the episodes, but every so often since Ava's death she felt as if she'd changed tracks and was ten or a hundred or a thousand parallel lives over from the life she had started out on. She went to bed on one track and woke up on another very much like the last, identical as far as she was concerned, all the inconsistencies having been addressed in sleep. Imperfectly addressed, of course, or there wouldn't be these moments.

AUGUST 1982

Rose dreamed that Gordon's truck jostled up the dirt road between their backyard and the neighbor's mustard field. It was a way of approaching the barn without being seen from the house. He swung onto their property and stopped. Dread sifted through her even before he pushed open the passenger door and Ava appeared from behind the barn and climbed in. Off they drove, continuing northward.

She woke with a lurch. She walked next door to Ava's room, shivering and still frightened, and stood near the bed to establish the rise and fall of her sister's chest. Shame at how she'd been treating Ava, combined with the fastidious demands of resentment, kept her from getting in under the covers. Back in her own bed she surrendered to what she'd known for days: Shannon wasn't coming. Asking her to phone had been a mistake. Repulsive people asked, magnetic people waited.

She and Ava returned to how they'd been, except Rose was listless and sad. She felt demoted, having to play with her little sister after learning how to identify native plants and build a lean-to with an older girl who was a genius and had the third eye. She often thought about the lean-to. It wasn't an exercise in anguish, because she removed Shannon from the picture. She saw herself collecting the branches on her own, arranging them, stuffing ferns into the cracks. She imagined equipping the interior with a plate and cup and spoon, a bottle of water, peanut butter and bread, a knife, a flashlight, her sketchbook and her colored pencils. Everything a person needed she would have in that tiny shelter of her own making.

There were no ferns anywhere near their property and no branches that their father hadn't broken up and thrown onto the woodpile. One cool, gray morning in late August, with Ava trailing along and asking what they were doing, Rose searched the roadsides between their farm and the next concession over. They found nothing, only a rotten red-and-white pole, like a barber pole.

On the way back Rose told Ava about the lean-to, and after recovering from the fact that Rose had gone to the other side of the cornfield, Ava said, "What about the planks in the loft?"

Rose wanted to take them from that filthy room to the meadow behind the barn, but Ava wasn't able to carry her end. By herself Rose lugged one as far as the doors, where, arms aching, she had to put it down.

"We better ask Gordon," Ava said.

"Why?"

"It's his wood. He might not like it getting rained on."

"This is Gordon's wood?"

"He's storing it."

Rose dragged the plank back.

She found a broom down below and spent the rest of the morning sweeping the dirt and rodent turds into piles, and Ava—bravely, for her—whisked the piles into a dustpan and deposited them outside. At lunch Rose told Fiona what they were up to. Fiona saw no reason why they couldn't borrow Gordon's wood, not to lean against the wall, though. "You'll knock them over," she said. "You'll brain yourselves." She had another idea. She went with the girls to the barn, and she and Rose created two solid stacks of different heights. They'd brought a couple of worn chenille bedspreads and they draped one across the planks to serve as a slanted roof. The other they bunched on the floor. They'd also brought supplies—a deck of cards, apples, grape juice boxes, and a bag of almonds. Only when Fiona said to Ava, "You'll be all right?" did Rose remember that Ava was claustrophobic.

"I'll be at the door part," Ava said. Fiona left, and she revised that to, "I'll stay out here and guard."

"There's lots of space," Rose assured her. There was *too much* space. And too much light, the depthless, dreary light of a classroom. "We should have built it in the meadow," she said.

"I like having it here," Ava said. She crouched down.

"Then come in."

"I like it for *you*."

"Don't you want to have a spirit vision?"

"What's a spirit vision?"

Rose was only trying to dredge up a little atmosphere. But as she answered Ava, she got that sensation she'd had with Shannon, of a mist falling on her arms, and she said, "Come right now, the vision's starting," and Ava let herself be pulled in.

"Okay, settle down, close your eyes," Rose said. She took Ava's hand. "It's the year 1786," she said, hushing her voice. "We're Oneida Indian sisters. We have jobs. We pick blueberries. We gather kindling for the fire."

She saw the fire: a tepee of logs, and the black, whipping smoke.

"What's that smell?" Ava said.

"There's no smell."

"Like vegetable soup."

"That's our campfire," Rose said, although she didn't smell anything.

"No, it's like . . ." Ava freed her hand and scrambled out. "It's like Campbell's vegetable soup."

Rose kept her eyes shut. She strained to preserve the smoke but it was narrowing to a strand.

"Are you still having the vision?" Ava asked timidly.

"No."

"Did I ruin it?"

"I probably wasn't having one anyway," Rose said. "You need to be in the bush." She crawled out and stood. "Well, that's that," she said, looking down at the windows, the source of all the light. A few of the panes were broken, and fluffy gray feathers quivered in the cracks. This must have been a chicken coop, she thought. She had the most dismal feeling.

"Oh, I know!" Ava blurted. She ran gawkily to the cupboard. "I'll have my lean-to here. It's even leaning." The door opened with a wail. "We'll each have our own one," she said and tucked herself into the bottom shelf.

Rose went over and looked at her sister's petrified, grinning face beaming up out of the impossible folds and angles of her limbs. "What do you think you're do-ing?" she said. "This is smaller than what we have."

"But it doesn't smell bad," Ava said. "It smells nice." Her freckles were vivid against her white skin. "You can shut the door."

"Get out of there."

"You can shut the door."

Rose shut the door.

She left the room.

"Are you in your lean-to?" Ava called. "Rose?"

A plump male pigeon and a slender female were strutting in front of Gordon's shingles, making their bubbling coos. The wind whistled. The windmill creaked. Rose walked around the barn to the meadow and swam her hands over the goldenrod and Queen Anne's lace. When she returned, the pigeons flapped up to a beam.

She never remembered what happened after that. She was told what happened, the details it was decided she should know or could tolerate. She overheard certain things between her parents and the forensic team, and years later she read the police and coroner reports, and learned that at 1:45 she used the hose to top up Major Tom's water tub. This was a regular chore, and Fiona, passing through the kitchen on her way to the cellar, witnessed it. The time of death was put at 1:30, so Rose might have already discovered the toppled cupboard, pulled Ava's lifeless body free, and covered her with the chenille bedspreads.

Roughly two hours later Fiona found Rose drawing in her sketchbook on the living room carpet. She asked where Ava was, and Rose apparently related the dream she'd had a week or so earlier, telling it as if it had really happened: Gordon driving up the dirt road behind the house, stopping by the barn and opening the passenger door, Ava jumping in, the two of them continuing on north.

Fiona called Gordon's home. Nobody answered. She called his wife at the Honda plant to get the number for his pager, but the wife had left work early. She called Rose's father, who called the police and began the hour-and-a-half drive from Toronto. The police issued an all-points bulletin. An RCMP squad car with two officers, a man and a woman, showed up within fifteen minutes.

Rose's answers were described in the police report as definite. She herself was described as mature for her age and reasonably calm and collected. She had entered a state of shock, but no one, least of all her, realized it at the time and therefore nobody doubted her, this reasonably calm and collected child with her definite answers. She told the police she'd left to give Major Tom his water, and when she got back, Ava wasn't there. She heard Gordon's truck and looked out the windows. "The loft windows," she said in an unconscious modification of her dream. She said that she didn't think Gordon saw her looking out, and that she felt funny about Ava driving away with him but guessed he must have phoned their mother first. No, Ava never mentioned Gordon coming to get her.

The policewoman asked the questions. She wanted Rose to take her to the loft and show her the view from the windows. Rose volunteered to draw a picture of the view instead. A second squad car arrived. Only minutes later Gordon pulled up in his truck.

One day Rose would mark the sight of that truck parked at an angle on the grass as the moment she returned to life. The male and female pigeons flapped to the barn roof, and the next thing she knew she was in the house and her face was pressed to the torn screen door with its rusty metal smell. There were police cars, and policemen putting Gordon in handcuffs. Why? What had he done? He wasn't resisting, he was saying to Fiona, "I didn't take her. I swear to you, I didn't take her." His round, pink face. His wobbling chin. "Why would I be here if I took her?" He appealed to the officers, looking left and right, landing left. "Tommy, come on, man, why would I be here?"

"You tell us," said the officer to his right. He wore mirrored sunglasses.

"That's what I'm doing!"

"You drove up the dirt road," said Fiona. She was half the size of the policemen. From the back, in her painting shift, she could have been Ava. "You stopped at the barn."

"I never use that road," Gordon pleaded.

"We have to take him in for questioning, ma'am," said the officer with the sunglasses.

"Question him here," Fiona said.

"Sorry, ma'am, can't do that. We'll keep you posted up to the minute."

They started leading Gordon to the squad car. He balked. "Hold on, Tommy. I got to scratch my head. I'm going crazy, man. It's the cancer."

The officers looked at each other.

"You scratch it for me, then."

The one named Tommy unclipped the hard hat, removed it, and there was Gordon's bald pink skull and the dent. Tommy hesitated. "Where do you want it?"

"All over."

Tommy used his knuckles.

"You drove up the dirt road," Fiona said, starting over.

Gordon shut his eyes to soak up the scratching.

"Listen to me!" Fiona screamed.

His eyes flew open. Tommy dropped his hand.

"You drove up the dirt road," Fiona said, not screaming but shrill. "You stopped at the barn. You opened the passenger door." Each action punctuated with a stab at the air. "Ava got in."

Rose started to shake. Having blanked out everything she'd said and done for the past three hours, she couldn't understand how her mother could be telling her dream. She went out onto the stoop, and the policewoman put a hand on her shoulder and tried to escort her back inside.

"Let's get you something to drink," said this woman.

Rose held her ground. "Are they talking about Ava?" she asked, although she knew they were.

"We'll find her, sweetie. Don't you worry."

"But she's in the loft."

"What did you say?"

"Ava's in the loft. She's in the cupboard."

⚭

Gordon died of his cancer a month later. Rose's father went to the funeral, making the trip from Toronto, where he, Fiona, and Rose, the shrunken family, were living again. Filtered down to Rose was the understanding that Gordon's death had been accelerated by the hour during which local news stations and CB radio operators had connected him to a missing young girl. Also that his death was a minor casualty, a small thing compared.

To Rose it was nothing. There was only the one death. She sobbed and thrashed in her father's arms. "You wouldn't have shut the door!" she cried. "You wouldn't have left!"

He said he would have. The latch was broken, he reminded her. "Ava could have pushed it open if she'd wanted to."

"She did want to! That's why it fell over!"

"We'll never know why it fell over. She died instantly. She didn't suffer."

Fiona, rocking herself nearby, begged Rose to stop: "No more, no more," she said.

Another time Fiona said, "When I was twelve, I threw a brass vase at my brother and cracked his skull open."

This helped somewhat, temporarily. But her mother threw the vase in a fit of temper. Rose shut the door in a fit of calm. She couldn't tell this one thing, it was too evil and, in any case, indescribable: the luxurious feeling that came over her as she walked away. How easy and funny it was, floating off, ignoring Ava's trusting, "Are you in your lean-to?"

SUNDAY, JULY 3, 2005

Rose prayed for Marsh to be at the yoga center. She appealed to God, and then—it felt more straightforward
and promising—she routed the prayer through Harriet.
Tell him not to leave, tell him to wait, she said, a variation
of the same words she'd directed at Harriet six hours
earlier.

She made it five minutes before closing time. The
doors were already locked. She pounded on the glass.
"Hello!" she shouted. "Hello! Open up!"

"They won't be opening up," said a raspy male voice.
It came from a figure in a wheelchair. "You can yell till
you're blue in the face." He pushed himself closer. He
was old and black, and missing a leg.

Rose pointed to a second-floor window. "A light's on."

"They all done for the day," he said heavily, as if speaking for himself.

Maybe there was a buzzer or entry panel. She felt around the doorframe. "You don't happen to have a key, do you?"

"Me?" He took the question seriously. "No, I don't have a key." He wheeled over to her and turned up his palm. "Are you going to help me out?"

Aside from a fifty, all she had in her purse was two quarters. She gave them to him.

"Do you need that watch?" he said.

"Pardon?"

He nodded at her wrist.

"It isn't real." Her real Rolex, her father's Rolex, she reserved for industry events. "It's a knockoff."

"That's all right." He turned up his palm again, and in her distraction, her bewilderment about what was expected, she pulled the watch off and gave it to him.

"Try the back door," he said.

She ran on the soaking lawn between the yoga center and a parking garage. Surely, they wouldn't have left the back door open.

But they had.

There were no stairs down, however, no obvious way to reach the basement offices. She climbed to the second level and entered a narrow hall of darkened rooms. The door to the first room was open. She peeked in. A massage table, a sink. She kept going. Light shone from the window of a closed door farther along. She drew closer and heard what she thought was crying. She tiptoed. She told herself she shouldn't look but, of course, she did.

A large naked man was bent over a table, legs braced, hips moving. Beneath him, legs in the air, lay another naked man. It was this man who was crying out. The standing man was Marsh.

Rose gasped and stepped aside. Was she in her own body? Yes, these were her hands, her shoes.

She could still say it, she could tap on the door, get Marsh to come out, and tell him what she'd rehearsed in the car: "Harriet tried to drown herself this afternoon. I saw her, I was really close. I know this sounds crazy, but just call her." She would then turn and leave. But Marsh might come after her, grab her arm, demand to know why she was following Harriet.

Better to write a note, she decided. She got out her pen and felt around in her purse for a scrap of paper. Meanwhile, the man's cries grew louder.

She lost her nerve.

To avoid the legless guy, she circled around the other side of the building. She was whimpering at her failure and her violation of Marsh's privacy. Between Harriet and him she was seeing too much, more than she had any right to see. And she'd been sure that he was in love with Harriet! Well, there went any hope of him marrying her and adopting the baby.

She reminded herself, driving off, that Harriet had chosen *not* to drown. When she felt more confident about this, she started questioning her mania to bring Marsh into the picture. If she'd actually spoken to Marsh, and he'd spoken to Harriet . . . Only now did it strike her how disturbed Harriet would be to learn that a stranger was interfering so diligently in her life.

Traffic was slow. Between the Bayview Extension and Pottery Road it stopped altogether, and an ambulance screamed past on the shoulder. She phoned the theater's kitchen line. Lloyd answered, and she explained the situation.

"Everything's under control here," he said. "No rush."

She spent the next hour reviewing the episodes, moment by moment, for anything else she might have gotten as wrong as assuming Marsh was heterosexual. But the moments wouldn't bind together, they had the jerky animation of a flipbook, and she kept returning to the first and starting over.

It was eleven thirty when she arrived at the theater. Her mother was in the kitchen, drinking tea and reading the newspaper.

"Where's Lloyd?" Rose said.

"He came down with a migraine and didn't have his pills. I sent him home."

"He was fine when I called."

"Migraines hit all of a sudden."

"They can," said Rose, making note of another coincidence. Not that she'd had a migraine, but a migraine specter had been haunting the theater for days.

"I called him a taxi," Fiona said. "He wanted to take the bus, but I wouldn't hear of it. And then he wouldn't let me give the driver any money." She sounded gratified. Lloyd the martyr, Lloyd the gentleman. "Do we know a Henry Corrigan?" she asked.

"*I* don't," Rose said. She went over to the sink.

"Henry will be missed by his many friends at Dunkin' Donuts," Fiona read in the derisive voice she reserved for the obituaries. "Well, that explains his heart attack."

Rose opened the cupboard. "Where's the purse?"

Their arrangement was, if Rose couldn't make it back to the theater by the end of the second show, Fiona would count the money and stick it in the leather cash purse, as she'd always done, but instead of maddening herself by trying to remember the combination to the safe, she would hide it under the sink behind the cleansers and detergents. Preferably, she would do this without Lloyd seeing.

"I put it in the safe," she said. "My hand automatically turned the combination."

Rose twisted around. "Mom!" she congratulated her.

"Oh, I'll forget again tomorrow."

"How did we do?"

"Thirty-five seventy-five from the snack bar, and a hundred and forty, no, two hundred and seventy . . ."

"I'll go see."

The safe was in the utility closet, embedded in the floor and walls. It was as old as the building. It was open. It was empty.

A film of sweat coated Rose's skin. She touched her wrist. She had given the legless man her fake twenty-dollar Rolex, and her real, fifteen-thousand-dollar Rolex had disappeared. For a moment she seemed to grasp an occult, inviolable law. But everything was gone: her father's diamond cuff links, Fiona's diamond-and-emerald anniversary ring, the night's take.

She returned to the kitchen and opened more cupboards. She shoved aside pots and pans.

"You're making a terrible racket," Fiona said.

"The safe is empty."

"What do you mean, empty?"

"There's nothing in it."

"That can't be," Fiona said. She got up and left the room. Coming back, she made for the fridge. "Sometimes I put things in the freezer," she muttered.

Rose stood with her hands on her hips. She was remembering Lloyd's "How high?" when she'd said she gambled online. His "No rush." She found his cell number on the bulletin board. "Was Lloyd still here when you opened the safe?" she asked her mother.

"Why? Who are you calling?"

"Lloyd." She got a rapid busy signal and hung up. "He robbed us. Thank God we're insured."

"What are you talking about?"

"He suddenly comes down with a migraine. He leaves and doesn't tell me. His phone isn't working."

"Lloyd would never rob us," Fiona said, appalled.

"The safe is empty."

"That's me." Fiona rapped her chest. "I did it."

"You took everything out of the safe?"

"I did."

"Where did you put it? Not in here."

Fiona opened the oven.

"I'm calling the police," Rose said.

"The police!"

"Mom, we've been robbed."

Fiona snatched the receiver and slammed it in the cradle. "We are not calling the police," she said with quavering ferocity. "We've called the police on an innocent man before."

Did she mean Gordon? Well, who else?

"I might have thrown everything out," Fiona said, composing herself. It was possible that she hadn't intended the reference to be so blunt, or even to let it slip. "Let's look."

They looked in the recycling bins. They looked in the snack bar and ticket booth. They switched on the houselights, and while Fiona poked around backstage among the old projectors and lobby chairs and film canisters and sheaves of mailing tubes with their vintage movie posters that Rose kept meaning to sell on eBay, Rose shined a flashlight under the seats. She did the same in the balcony. She searched the washrooms. She searched her office and the projection booth. All she'd done all day was search. This time she was going through the motions so that later she'd be able to remind Fiona that they'd looked everywhere. She called Lloyd's number again and got the rapid busy signal. She joined Fiona backstage and beamed her light down tunnels of rolled carpeting. By now Lloyd would be over the border. Rose imagined him in a wrecked car (he had only so much ready cash) on his way to Mexico (his skull tattoos), but against her mother's heroic exertions she said nothing. She would miss the Rolex.

A moment came when Fiona sank onto one of the chairs and kicked off her pumps. "If only I could remember what I was thinking," she said.

"You'll remember in the morning," Rose said, humoring her. Lloyd's absence tomorrow would speak for itself.

"Wait," Fiona said. She stood and walked determinedly in her stocking feet to the front of the screen.

Rose followed. "Mom," she groaned, "let's call it a night."

"Hold your horses," Fiona said. She descended the shallow steps to the orchestra pit and marched to the shelf beneath the stage.

"I looked there," Rose said.

But Fiona reached way in.

"I found it," she said, tense with achievement. She loosened the string and felt inside. "Everything's here." She gave the purse to Rose and went over to the stairs and sat. "And you thought it was Lloyd."

Rose opened and shut the jewelry cases. "Don't tell him," she said.

"*I* wouldn't tell him. Don't *you* tell him."

On the short drive to the house Fiona slept. Rose slowed for speed bumps and came to gradual stops. Never again would she trust Fiona with the cash purse, that was over. She would change the combination. She would wear the Rolex, and when she wasn't wearing it, she would hide it in her dresser drawer. What else? Unplug the stoves, they never used them anyway. Confiscate Fiona's car keys.

At home she told Fiona that she was having an early breakfast with their accountant. "I'll put your pills out," she said. "Sleep tight."

Rose herself was too wound up to sleep. She opened a bottle of wine and went into the living room to watch the Weather Network. Thundershowers at eleven tomorrow, an eighty percent chance as opposed to the ninety percent she'd grown accustomed to. A forty percent chance on Tuesday, twenty percent Wednesday. Clear on Thursday.

So, seventy-two hours at the outside, and then there would be an interval of however many days, weeks, months as she waited to learn from the next band of storms whether or not the episodes were over. They had better be over. All her berserk racing from one corner of the city to the other would kill her. It had almost killed her today. Her limbs began to tremble, and she drained her glass. *I hope you're asleep*, she said to Harriet, *after what you put us through.*

She returned to the kitchen, poured more wine, and drank it down. She rummaged through her purse and briefcase. Where were her cigarettes?

She walked. The car was low on gas, and you could get to the theater almost as quickly on foot. She didn't worry that Fiona would start wandering before daybreak. It had never happened. She brooded over Harriet's baby. Lately, every faint ticking noise—the car engine cooling, the dishwasher starting—was the baby's heartbeat.

In the lobby she turned on the wall sconces. And nearly tripped over a folded sleeping bag and two lumpy pillows. The brothers was her first thought.

It wasn't them, although they were smoking with Lloyd outside the kitchen door. The tall one spotted her and raised his hand.

Lloyd glanced around. "Hey, Rose," he said. "Everything okay?"

The brothers slipped away like cats.

"I left my cigarettes upstairs," she said. It was jarring to see him after how close she'd come to calling the police. He offered his cigarette. "Thanks," she said and took a puff.

"Keep it," he said.

A brown leather carryall and his tobacco pouch were on the table. "Is that your sleeping bag in the lobby?" she asked.

"Yeah, sorry. My cell died, or I'd have checked if I could crash here, just for the night. I get home, and the people in the apartment above me are having a monster blowout."

"Where's your daughter?"

"With her mother." He saw Rose looking at the bottle of Crown Royal on the counter. "Fiona probably told you, I came down with a migraine."

"How is it?"

"The pills work. In combination. Can I pour you a drink?"

She hated whisky. It was after one o'clock, and she wanted to be at Harriet's office tomorrow before eight. "Sure," she said.

He passed her the jar lid that served as his ashtray. "Water? Ice?"

"Ice."

"Ice it is."

Her desire for men had always been predicated on some aspect of their circumstances or history she could feel sorry for. This wasn't that. There was nothing pitiful about Lloyd. This was all his years, all the other women he'd been with, his chin deflating into pleats when he looked down, his prison record. Or so she told herself. She pulled out her mother's chair. "You're welcome to sleep here every night," she said, closing the obituary pages. "Free security for us."

"We'll see how many parties they have, but thanks." He brought over the drinks, and she started in on hers. He sat across from her and began rolling a cigarette, making a filter first, which he placed on the end of a second paper. His pinch of tobacco was exactly enough. He plucked out a bud.

Watching a certain type of deft manual activity sent Rose into the same state of sensual bliss she got when somebody combed her hair. She had that feeling now. "They could have warned you," she said.

"Normally, it wouldn't have bothered me. But with a migraine. Have you ever had one?"

Interesting question. "I thought I had a silent migraine once."

"Silent migraine."

"You get the aura and light sensitivity but you miss the headache."

"Kind of like what other people call a buzz."

"Well, scarier. So how'd you get here? Did you take a taxi?"

"No, I took advantage of an opportunity. I was trying to sleep in this girl's car. She'd left it unlocked—"

"She'd left it unlocked!"

"Actually, she'd left the keys on the seat."

"That's not smart."

He licked the paper's glue strip. "Anyway, it smelled like dead dog in there, even with all the windows down, so I think, wait a minute, I can drive off."

"You drove off?"

"Parked right outside."

She put down her glass. "Did you tell the girl?"

He smiled and dug a lighter out of the front pocket of his jeans. "Rose, you think the worst of me."

"No, I don't." But she did. Forget earlier this evening, a few days ago she'd nearly accused him of drugging her coffee. "Okay, you told her."

"She's someone I hang out with occasionally. And no, I didn't tell her. She was"—a pause to light the cigarette—"unavailable."

"Hang out with" sounded like have sex with. "Unavailable" sounded like having sex. "Unavailable how?"

"Passed out."

"From what?"

"Shots. Weed. Partying. I told her friend."

"She shouldn't be driving," Rose said, glad for a reason to reproach the competition. "You might have saved her life."

"There you go."

They smoked their cigarettes. Rose coughed. "My virgin throat," she said.

"You're a late bloomer."

"I've never smoked weed, either," she said, hoping he would take care of that as well. He watched her. He wasn't about to comment. "Pathetic," she said. "Right?"

"What's pathetic about it?"

"You wouldn't happen to have any on you."

Back came the smile.

"That's not me thinking the worst. That's me wanting to party. For a change."

He reached for her glass. "Refill?"

"Oh. Sure."

"You don't party?"

"Hardly ever. I've always been scared of letting go. Getting lost. These past few days, though, let me tell you, I've—" She stopped herself. She was talking too much. "Thanks," she said, accepting her glass.

"You're welcome."

"What about LSD?"

"What about it?"

"Have you tried it?"

"You're talking to an old hippie."

"What's it like?"

"Acid?" He tilted his chair back. "As I recall, it's like reality turned up a hundred percent. Everything amplified, but real."

"Has it ever, I mean, did you ever . . ." She crushed her cigarette in the jar lid. "When you were on acid did you ever feel like you were inside someone else? Inside their body?"

"That isn't how psychedelics work, not in my experience anyway. You're you, it's your body. You always know that much."

"Okay." She had hoped she might be on to something, a chemical angle. She shut her eyes from a sense of herself in outer space and the earth receding. "I should lie down," she said.

She went to the lobby, got his sleeping bag and pillows, and dragged them to the concession, out of sight of the front doors. She unfolded the bag and lay on her back.

He tucked a pillow under her head. "Is this the whisky?"

"I had wine at home. I'm not much of a drinker. Jeez, these are crappy pillows."

"You might be more comfortable in your office. On your couch."

"I'm fine." She took off her glasses, which, for her, was like taking off her blouse. "Why don't you sit beside me?"

He squatted, knees cracking.

"Sit on the other pillow," she said.

He did, and she patted his boot, acknowledging its proximity to her hand. After a moment she found herself stroking the rough, wedge-shaped toe between her thumb and fingers. Was this as sexy for him as it was for her? "You know what?" she said, getting herself upright. "I'm better vertical." Their arms touched. She looked at him. He smiled. She zeroed in on his lips.

"Not a good idea," he said, leaning back.

"Victor and I broke up."

"You're my boss. I like this job."

"Right. You're absolutely right." How mortifying.

He retrieved her glasses. He helped her stand and jogged upstairs for her cigarettes. He couldn't do enough for her. He offered to walk her home but she said, "No way," and laughed and said, "You're fired," and then, "I'm kidding, I'm kidding."

"I'll see you out," he said.

Under the marquee he lit a cigarette. She fluttered her fingers—*Bye!* Suffering his gaze on her bum was what she got for renouncing Victor, making their breakup sound permanent. But it *was* permanent, she thought. And then she realized that Victor had already figured this out. It was why when she'd said, "Until then," he'd said nothing.

MONDAY, JULY 4, 2005

The car needed gas, and Rose wasn't sure where to park around King and University. She called a taxi. While waiting for it, she wrote her mother a note: *Mom, I've gone to my breakfast meeting. You aren't on a cruise ship. Open the front door and go out to the porch if you don't believe me! xx.* She put the note on the toilet seat lid and took another Advil for her hangover.

At eight o'clock she was stationed near the elevators in the lobby of Harriet's building. By eight fifteen she was back on the sidewalk, smoking, monitoring the subway exit.

The Indian-print dress she'd worn on Thursday she now judged to have been too flamboyant. This morning she wore a cream-colored cotton blouse and a plain dirndl skirt, greenish blue, the same color as the Advils. She knew what she was going to say. It wasn't what she wanted to say. She wanted to confess everything she'd seen and heard and felt inside Harriet's body from the first phone call on Wednesday afternoon to the exchange with Fiona at the snack bar. But she could hardly do that. She would keep it to a brief, half-truthful, unalarming, "Excuse me, Harriet Smith? Hi, I'm Rose Bowan from the Regal Theater. My mother told me she had a lovely talk with you the other night. We actually met, you and I, a couple of years ago at a book launch"—to explain how Rose recognized her. "I don't want to hold you up, it's just I've brought my father's manuscript, and I promised my mother I'd give it to you personally."

Of course, a conversation wasn't essential. But to be addressed by that croaky voice, to watch the lips move.

Eight twenty. The receptionist hustled by with her severe hair and scowl. Eight thirty. Rose sat on the edge of a concrete planter and lifted her feet to let an elderly cleaner sweep her cigarette butt into a pan. "Sorry," she said. He nodded. His face was as indiscriminately lined as a breadboard, whereas the lines on a face like Lloyd's were organized and readable: smile lines, crow's-feet. *Not a good idea.* She cringed. What had she been thinking? She was as bad as her mother. Maybe their mutual attraction to Lloyd pointed to another coincidence, in this case one provoked not only by the psychic fallout of the episodes but also by the massive uproar of Fiona's dementia—two grand, mind-altering events crossing paths at the nexus of their ex-hippie, ex-drug-using employee.

Eight forty. She wondered if the building had another entrance and went back inside. And on the wall between the third and fourth elevators, somehow invisible to her earlier, was a parking garage sign.

The subway is a hundred feet from your office, and you drive? she berated Harriet. She dug out her cell and called Goldfinch.

"May I ask who's calling?" said the receptionist.

"I'm from the Canada Council for the Arts," said Rose.

"She's on another line. Would you like to hold?"

Rose hung up. Harriet was there. But how to get to her?

The answer came seconds later. An elevator opened, and David stepped out and strode past her and into the coffee shop. She waited, heart jumping, collecting herself, strategizing. When he reappeared, he was frowning at his phone. "David, hi," she said.

He looked over. "Hi," he said, clearly unable to place her.

"Rose. We met last Thursday. You told me where the washrooms were."

"Rose from the Regal." He produced a smile. Until now she hadn't spared a thought for how he might be feeling about having had to end things with Harriet. "Up?" he asked and pressed the button.

"Up. Yes."

He returned to his cell.

"Goldfinch is considering publishing my father's book," she said.

His gaze slid over. "Really?"

They entered the elevator behind three other people. "It's a history of the Regal and his forty-five years at the helm."

David nodded. "Okay."

"Not many people know that it started out as a vaudeville theater." She had to keep him talking so that the receptionist would think they were together. "In 1894."

"It's that old, eh?"

She moved to let a person off. "There were all sorts of incredible acts back then. Aerialists, gigantic human pyramids, a guy who could juggle seven flaming torches."

At some point she would have to mention Harriet in order to find her office. He saved her the trouble: "Who's your editor?"

"Harriet Smith."

"Harriet." He rubbed his jaw. "Interesting."

He kept rubbing his jaw. Rose felt her cheeks flush, and she looked down. His fingers had smelled of oranges. "I remember you saying how you love our cupola," she went on. "Well, it nearly didn't get built. The architect was this prima donna." She chattered away. They arrived, crossed the reception area, and made it unchallenged to the hall. "So," she said. "Harriet is . . ."

He nodded over her shoulder. "Hang a left, halfway down. There's a poster of Virginia Woolf on the door."

"Right. Thank you."

He raised his coffee cup.

One of her recurring early-childhood dreams was of walking in a state of hypnotic expectation down a long, carpeted corridor. Since Thursday, if you counted the thin runner at Fruit of Life, she'd been living this dream every day.

Virginia Woolf's wan smile brought her to a halt. *You don't have to do this*, it seemed to say. *Nobody's holding a gun to your head.*

The door was ajar. Rose took the last few steps and knocked. "Hello?" She nudged the door wider.

It was like pulling the trigger and getting a click. It was like a blinding camera flash, her disbelief that

Harriet wasn't there, her inability to see it. Out of the fading splotches before her eyes, the windows and desk and bookcases from her first episode emerged. She told herself that Harriet must have gone out for a minute, but nothing like a newspaper or a coffee cup or any sort of disorder indicated recent habitation. She went to the front of the desk and opened the bottom drawer.

"May I help you?"

A man stood in the doorway. He had a lime-green bow tie and a meringue of blond hair.

"I'm looking for a pen," Rose said, staying calm. The drawer—it contained only hanging files—she shut with her knee.

"Editors *never* have pens," the man said. He patted the two ballpoints clipped to his shirt pocket. "Or pencils. They absolutely never have *red* pencils."

Rose moved away from the desk. "I'm supposed to be meeting Harriet. I thought I'd write her a note."

"She's in an editorial scrum. Would you like me to extract her?"

"Could you?" *I apologize for being devious*, she rehearsed.

"Who shall I say is going through her drawers?"

Rose smiled—she hoped she smiled. "Rose from the Regal Theater."

He raised his index finger. "Let me see what I can do."

She made as though to sit, but when she heard his voice down the hall, she went back to the desk and opened the top drawer. Pens and pencils, a *red* pencil, paperclips, rubber bands, scissors, a staple remover, all neatly arranged in a tray. She lifted the tray. Hand lotion, a travel-sized bottle of Listerine, a bottle of Tylenol Extra Strength. The next drawer had envelopes and letterhead. She looked around the room. There were manuscripts in tidy piles on the window ledge and credenza. On the bookshelves were photographs of the cats. Otherwise, the office was as impersonal as an Ikea office.

The clouds appeared to be darkening, but the windows were tinted, so it could have been an illusion. Rose sat in one of the guest chairs. She shut her eyes. Last night she'd slept two hours. Her right leg had a tremor, and she got out the manuscript and planted it on her knee. She opened the manuscript to a middle page. "Following the pony act," she read, "Heinrich would return to his dressing room and consult his crystal ball for the benefit of any stagehand or performer willing to pay the ten-cent fee. With few exceptions his prophecies were a variation on the theme that there are obstacles and afflictions on the road ahead, but there are also stretches of peace and contentment. This being a truth applicable to nearly every life ever lived, every story ever told, every movie ever made, Heinrich gained a reputation in the theatrical community for mystical accuracy"—

"Well," drawled the bow-tied man, suddenly at the door. "It seems that Harriet has come and gone."

"What?" She closed the manuscript. "Already?"

"People come and go so quickly here," he said in a stagey voice. She stared at him. He reverted to brisk concern. "Would you like to speak to her executive assistant?"

How had Rose missed her? "Is she coming back?"

"Possibly. I could have the receptionist call her if you like."

"I can call her, if you give me the number."

"My dear, it's a hanging offense to give out an editor's number."

Rose put the manuscript in her briefcase. She stood. She had the disquieting impression of being duped: David and Marsh, this character, they were all on to her. "Thanks for your help," she said.

"Is there anything—" A loud thunderclap startled them both. "Oh, my sainted aunt," he said.

She walked away, the wrong way, she discovered, upon turning a corner and finding herself in a storage area of desks and tables and unassembled shelving. The shelving brackets glowed. The flecks appeared and began their nauseating choreography. She crouched under a desk, and then she lay down.

⏾

She was urinating into a plastic cup, skirt bunched in her free hand, the mauve shoulder bag, with an umbrella sticking out of it, hanging on the back of the door. Above the toilet paper dispenser a framed sign said, PLEASE NOTIFY FRONT DESK IF TOILET BLOCKS.

Increase the water pressure, thought Rose, who owned and maintained sixteen toilets and was trying not to believe that these circumstances amounted to anything other than a regular appointment with Harriet's family doctor or obstetrician.

Harriet's mood was somber. Washing her hands, she disregarded the mirror and gazed at her murky reflection in the faucet. She wiped the outside of the cup with a wet paper towel and used a dry towel to protect her clean hand when she opened the door. The grandmotherly woman behind the front desk relieved her of the cup and said, "Now, if you'll take a seat in the waiting room."

All the seats except one were occupied. To reach it she had to step over the stretched-out legs of a scrawny young guy picking his face and filling out a questionnaire. His girlfriend rubbed her forehead on his shoulder and murmured answers.

Nobody was old. None of the women were obviously pregnant. She sat next to a woman flossing her teeth behind her hand. The windows were too high to see out of, but you could hear the rain. She picked up *Cottage Life* magazine and glanced at the subscription sticker—Toronto Women's Health.

Oh, no, Rose thought. Last year she'd attended a fund-raising dinner for Toronto Women's Health, a two-hundred-dollar-a-plate affair, lots of speeches, and a film about back-street abortions over the closing credits of which she was moved to say to the woman beside her, "I've never been so glad I had a hysterectomy," and the woman, a middle-aged police officer, gave Rose's arm a congratulatory pat and said, "You're off the hook."

Not quite off.

She put the magazine down. She seemed to have two pulses: a slow thud in her chest and a surface flutter in her stomach. How could Harriet bear it? *Get out of here*, Rose said. The slow heartbeat quickened promisingly, but then it began to pound. *Go, go*, Rose begged.

Harriet was keeping her turmoil private. She was pushing her hands together, taking short, soft breaths.

"Excuse me, would you happen to have any gum?" said the woman with the dental floss, and Rose was back inside her own body.

☩

She got herself out from under the desk and found the corridor. Behind her the voice of the bow-tied man called, "Are you lost?" She walked more purposefully. She reached a T-junction, spotted an exit sign, and escaped.

She'd had girlhood dreams about this, too: racing down a concrete stairwell, sobbing. The baby wasn't hers, it wasn't Ava's, she knew that. It wasn't the life that was going to exonerate her for Ava's death.

But you get attached.

The rear ground-floor exit opened onto an alley. She jogged through light rain to Richmond Street, where a row of taxis waited outside the Hilton.

"Toronto Women's Health," she told the driver. "I don't have the address."

He wedged into traffic. "It's up by Humber River Hospital."

"I'm in a bit of a hurry."

"Fifteen minutes, twenty, depends."

She listened for thunder, although the rain was letting up. Still, in the unthinkable event that she had an episode, she said, "I might fall asleep." The driver glanced at her in his mirror. Did he know what went on at Toronto Women's Health? She looked out her window.

Her vague strategy of hanging around on the sidewalk and following Harriet to her car crumbled as it dawned on her that you don't drive to your own abortion, you get driven in a taxi or by a friend. And you leave the same way. She considered Marsh, but only for a second. He didn't know about this, or else he'd have been in the waiting room. That was where Rose needed to get herself. If Harriet was already with the doctor, then Rose would linger over the questionnaire. She would vacillate, balk at the ultrasound, keep delaying until Harriet reappeared. She couldn't stop the abortion, it was too late for that, but she could at least see Harriet and attempt—psychically, at close range—to comfort her.

"Thirteen fifty," said the driver. He had pulled over next to a yellow-brick building with frosted first-floor windows and the high, square upper-floor windows from Rose's episode. "Smile, you're on TV," he said, making change, and she saw two cameras, one pointed straight down, one angled toward the road.

She saw a cloudbank tracking north. It might miss this part of town. Or it might not, and she would have an episode and stand every chance of entering Harriet during the abortion. She pictured her body drooped in a chair while, in Harriet's body, the commotion of people trying to revive her was audible. *Could* she be revived? She swayed through a backwash of dread. But she got out of the taxi and approached the clinic door. She pressed the buzzer.

"Yes?" said a female voice over the intercom.

"I'd like to speak to a counselor."

The door clicked open.

She expected a security guard and a search of her briefcase. But she was met by a short woman in a sari, a gray-haired South Asian woman who said only, "Follow me, please."

They passed shut doors and their silent interiors. Rose looked at the ceiling. Acoustic tiles. On top of those, plywood and insulation and mold-proofing—modern building strata unknown to her—and then a subfloor and then the carpet: a tan sisal that had felt rubbery beneath Harriet's feet.

The carpet down here was an Oriental runner. It led to a back office and a woman with white cotton hair behind a reception desk. This second woman detached herself from a computer screen. *Marion* was embroidered in cursive on her shirt pocket. Her blue eyes were kind. "Hello," she said. "What can I do for you?"

"Well, I'm here for the obvious reason," Rose said.

The woman in the sari folded her arms and leaned against the wall. A third woman, also up there in age, sat at a little round table and talked on the phone. Three old ladies—make that four, counting the one Harriet had given her urine sample to—intended, Rose presumed, to convey wisdom and homeness. Like midwives, except the opposite.

"When was your last period?" Marion asked.

"Eight weeks," Rose said, keeping it in the first trimester. She looked down. It was hard to lie to this person.

"Have you had a pregnancy test?"

"Yes."

Marion clasped her hands on the edge of her computer. "I'm obligated to tell you there are other options," she said.

"Not for me there aren't," Rose said. Her throat roughened, as if she spoke the truth.

"That's fine," Marion said gently. "Would you like to sit?"

"I'm okay."

"Our website, have you been to it?"

"Yes."

"So you know that past seven weeks it's a surgical procedure."

Rose didn't know. How pregnant was Harriet? Surely not seven weeks. "Yes," she said.

But she must have sounded doubtful because Marion said, "Before seven weeks, it's a medical procedure, meaning you take a pill, one here in the presence of the doctor and one a few days later on your own."

Rose nodded. At least Harriet wouldn't be sliced open. Or no, they used suction, didn't they? "Do you accept credit cards?" she asked.

"You don't pay," Marion smiled, happy, it seemed, to impart such unambiguously good news. "It's covered by Ontario health insurance."

"Not including any medication you may need afterward," cautioned the woman in the sari.

"On the day of your appointment, be sure to bring your health card," Marion said.

"No. No, I want it today. Now, actually."

"We don't do same-days," said the woman in the sari.

Marion peered at her screen. "I can get you in tomorrow morning. Eight o'clock."

"I can't come tomorrow." Rose thumped her briefcase on the chair, staking her claim. "I have to have it now."

"Eight weeks," said the woman in the sari. She shrugged. "A day or two won't make a difference."

"I took the morning off work."

"We're here on Saturdays from ten until six, and Sundays from noon until six," said Marion in the patient tone of a person who imparted this information regularly.

"I work every day, I work all the time," Rose said. Her bottom lip trembled. She did work every day and all the time.

"Other places do same-days," said the woman in the sari. She flicked her hand at these other places. "Not us."

Marion pushed a box of tissues closer to Rose. "You don't have to decide this very minute."

The woman in the sari led her back down the hall. Where were the stairs, behind which door? If Rose began opening doors, what was this old lady going to do about it?

But Rose did not open any doors.

The cameras—and a notion that hanging around abortion clinics was illegal—persuaded Rose to wait on the bench in front of the coffee shop across the street. She stepped off the curb, and a truck sped by and splashed her. It seemed deliberate. She thought that one of the ladies might rush out with towels. She even turned and looked into the camera lens. When nobody came, she made her way to the bench and wiped her arms and her Rolex with the soggy tissue she still clutched. The time was ten after ten. She should have asked Marion how long the whole procedure lasted, start to finish.

Wind shook the canopy above her and loosened streams of water onto the pavement. The cloudbank, visible over second-story rooftops, seemed stalled. She urged it closer. Now she *wanted* to be in Harriet when Harriet had the abortion, when she swallowed the pill. She wanted to apologize for her earlier panic and tell her she wasn't alone.

She told her anyway. She said, *You're a good person*, and *You have a right to be happy*, and other consoling, absolving things she had never believed when they'd been said to her but as she said them to Harriet she believed evangelically.

At twenty after ten a fat woman wearing pink jogging pants and a hoodie was let in. There followed a spate of activity: the dental floss woman leaving, the old lady from the waiting room hurrying off (on her break?), a girl in a private school uniform arriving, spotting the cameras, and hiking her jacket over her head.

At ten thirty a man lurched over and dropped down next to Rose. "You wouldn't happen to have a cigarette, would you?" he said. His face was a catastrophe of dents and open sores. Something yellow foamed out of the corner of his mouth. What was it about her lately that attracted these guys? She gave him a cigarette without any desire to smoke one herself. She sparked the lighter, and his hand came up expertly to cancel the wind. "Thank you kindly," he said.

Before the interruption she'd been speaking more intimately with Harriet, saying she knew about the suicide attempt. Now she admitted to having had a few suicidal thoughts of her own after Ava died, wishing it had been her instead of her sister. *But here I am, still in the world*, she said. *Glad I hung around.* Was she? Were her spells of gladness as authentic and satisfying as other people's? *I'm not saying I don't have my dark days. Life can be hard.* This last sentence she might have said out loud because the guy next to her, as if in passionate agreement, said, "Oh, *man!*"

He sank against her arm. She lifted the arm, and he sank onto her chest. "Sorry about that," he muttered, cigarette clamped between his lips. She shoved at the dead weight of him. He flailed and tried to wheel himself up.

Over his back she saw the shoulder bag before she saw the woman. "Move," she grunted desperately. Harriet was crossing the road.

He flailed again and knocked her glasses off. "I got 'em," he said. He had jerked himself into a sitting position and was dangling the glasses by one arm. She jumped to her feet. "Here you go," he said with a debonair wave of his wrist as the blur that was Harriet entered the coffee shop.

Where was the briefcase? Beneath his thigh. "Whoa, Nellie," he objected when she yanked it out from under him. "Hey, what are you . . ."

Harriet was at the counter, studying the pastries. Rose walked past, and that whole side of her tingled. She detoured to the condiment stand and wet some napkins and cleaned the mud off her legs. At this distance Harriet didn't seem as sharply pretty as she did in mirrors. She looked haggard, preoccupied. A server said, "Who's next?" and Harriet spoke, but Rose's pulse was deafening, and she heard only the server's "Blueberry?" He slapped a tray on the counter. On the tray he put a plate, and on the plate a muffin.

Rose searched for a table and managed to grab the only empty one before the couple ahead of Harriet got to it. Harriet went to the stand and poured milk into her coffee mug. Other single patrons were discouraging company with their backpacks and computers and impoverishment, one raggedy woman sound asleep and snoring. Rose put her briefcase on the table until the couple found seats. She got out the manuscript and opened it on her lap.

She turned a page, eyes lowered.

"Excuse me, is this chair taken?" That wonderful voice.

"No," Rose said. She glanced as high as Harriet's bitten nails. "No, it's free."

Harriet settled herself. She drank her coffee and took items from her purse. When Rose risked another glance, she was smoothing a newspaper folded to the crossword puzzle. The eyes, even downcast, were Ava's.

Don't cry, Rose ordered herself. If she started crying, she would never stop. She shifted her attention to the fingers as they went about their business, pulling apart the muffin, bringing chunks to the mouth, picking up the pen.

There must have been thunder. The lightning Rose confused with a perceptual short circuit that was twinkling Harriet in and out of focus, so that the flecks were also disguised. The manuscript fell off her lap.

℗

In Harriet's body, she bent to retrieve it. She straightened and beheld a large, disheveled woman, tangled hair, eyes closed: herself outside herself, the very sight she had feared in the theater when it had seemed that Harriet might enter her office and the both of them would die. But Harriet was alive, *she* was alive in Harriet, and "the woman" was at least upright.

She placed the manuscript on the table and touched the woman's arm. Her hand wasn't felt. "Are you all right?" she said. Incredibly, the woman nodded, a definite down, up, down. Who had heard the question? What *remained* of her to hear?

A smear of the guy's yellow foam sullied her blouse. Her glasses were crooked. Harriet was overcome with pity, so much pity that it overcame Rose. She had a sense that they were silently discussing her, saying that, after all, she wasn't so bad. Nice clothes, a shine to her hair, you wouldn't call her *unhealthy*. And wasn't that a Rolex? There they both were, inspecting her and feeling the most tender concern and love, forgiving her because it was obvious that she was the type of person who would never forgive herself.

Blood slid out of her nostril. They—Rose and Harriet—offered a napkin and were a single Harriet reflection in the woman's glasses. They put the napkin next to the manuscript. Might they get her something to drink? Coffee? Juice?

The woman shook her head.

"Okay, well," they said. "Take care." They stuck the pen and newspaper in the shoulder bag and transferred the cup and crimped muffin shell to the tray. They brought the tray to the counter and said, "Thank you." At the door they gave the woman a final worried look.

I'm in here forever, Rose thought.

①

She was in there for another second. She emerged crying and disoriented, her last dependable memory a glimpse of Harriet on the other side of the road. She wiped the blood and went outside and stood looking uncertainly at the clinic until a male server from the café dashed through the rain with her briefcase and manuscript. Her "Thank you," not in Harriet's voice but in her own, cleared her fog.

A taxi idled at the corner, and she climbed in and said, "The Regal Theater on Mount Pleasant."

"Is it too loud?" the driver asked about his music, country-and-western, a man singing that his bucket had a hole in it.

"No," said Rose. She was sweating under her drenched clothes, but she was alert now, and exuberant.

She itemized her experiences as if for a judge and jury. One: traveling day after day, sometimes twice a day, into the body of another woman, a pregnant woman. Two: seeing Harriet in the flesh. Three, and most astoundingly: seeing herself from outside herself.

The thunder reached her between songs. She gripped the leather strap above her window and stared at the license plate of the truck in front of them. She tried to recall the physical feeling of the last episode, but there were only emotions: hers, Harriet's, hers and Harriet's united.

Rain pitched down, lightning crackled on all sides. She looked out her window. Her vision wasn't sharpening. She blinked and rubbed her eyes. Nothing.

The episodes were over. Her whole body told her: a new kind of tension, the floating swoop you got when a plane loses altitude. The episodes were over. They stopped if the host body aborted a baby. They stopped if you saw yourself from outside yourself. They stopped because they stopped. Rose covered her face with her hands out of what felt like anguish and then, within a few minutes, like relief.

The thunder lost volume, the downpour lightened to rain, and the taxi pulled up outside the theater, her old faithful theater. She wondered if Lloyd had stayed on, but from the vestibule it was her mother she saw, moving around in the glowing pod of the snack bar.

"So you decided to make an appearance, did you?" Fiona said, her accent a blatant giveaway. She had been repositioning the drink cups. She switched, when Rose approached, to furiously scooping popcorn.

"You're early," Rose ventured.

"I'm late," Fiona snapped. Her face was pink. She wiped her forehead with the back of her arm. "Where's that man we hired?"

"It's a sauna in here," Rose said. It wasn't quite, but they were both overheated. She crossed to the electric panel and got the central air going.

"That's it, throw our money out the window," said Fiona.

"Look at the clock," Rose said. "Behind you."

"What for?"

"What time is it?"

Fiona twisted around. "Twelve," she said. She went still, ladle raised. "That can't be right," she said in her regular voice.

"Twelve noon," Rose said.

Fiona hung the ladle on its hook.

"Well, the popcorn's made," Rose said. "It'll keep."

"It will," Fiona said. "God help me."

"Why don't we sit inside?" Rose said. "Under the fans." She turned on the houselights.

"You're soaking wet," Fiona said and walked out from behind the counter.

"Oh, Mom," Rose said. From the waist down, except for her pumps, Fiona was naked. "Go back, go back," Rose said, making shooing motions. "What if Lloyd comes?"

"Who cares," Fiona said, but returned to her post.

"Where's your skirt?"

Fiona raised her eyes in one direction and limply pointed in the other, like a Leonardo da Vinci saint. Rose followed the finger to the ticket stand and a neat pile of clothing, underpants on top, an old lady's beige padded underpants. Her eyes stung. *I can't do this, it's too much*, she said to her father. *You're all abandoning me*, she said, and was once again a little girl at an agricultural fair, watching a man make cotton candy, turning to Ava and her parents, who should have been beside her, but they were far ahead, receding into the crowd.

"Rain, rain, rain," Fiona said cheerfully. "It's like the tropics."

Rose held up the skirt and underwear. "I need you to put these on," she said. "You can leave off your panty hose."

"Well, bring them here."

Barbara Gowdy

While her mother dressed, Rose opened the auditorium doors. She was thinking, home care, but who would Fiona tolerate? And how was Rose going to be able to tell when Fiona was suffering a ministroke if, half-naked, she could speak so sensibly and without an accent?

"Life is all doing and undoing," Fiona said. "Putting your clothes on, taking them off, dirtying the floor, washing the floor."

She wanted to sit in the front row. So they did, not directly under a fan, but it was cool enough.

"I haven't sat here since we bought the place," Fiona said, plucking the neck of her blouse.

They talked about the regulars who preferred the front row. There were six, they agreed, all of them young except for Gerry, who was eighty-something. Fiona came up with the names before Rose did. She was her old, quick self. Then she twisted around and said, impatiently, "Where's your father? Where's Ava?"

Yesterday Rose would have said, "Mom, they died." She would have dragged her back to the real world and their shared, incurable sorrows. Today she couldn't remember why she had ever found it necessary to be so remorseless.

"They'll be here," she said.

WEDNESDAY, SEPTEMBER 6, 2006

It was a lovely, clear, early-autumn morning, all the leaves still green, the rosebushes in second bloom. Rose had filled the bird feeder and mowed the lawn. Enid, the Filipina caregiver, had washed Fiona's hair and helped her dress.

Charles had come by as he came by every morning, weather permitting, so that he and Fiona could watch *Let's Make a Deal* together. Fiona called him Blackie, to Rose's horror, although Charles was fine with it. He called himself Blackie. He said, "Fiona, Blackie is here," and removed the white panama or gray homburg he wore just for the short trip across the road. Fiona waved him over to the sofa and patted his fleshless thigh, and he took her hand and entwined it in his gnarly, branchy fingers.

Barbara Gowdy

Now, at ten thirty, Rose, Fiona, and Enid were walking along College Street from the parking lot to the neurologist's. Fiona, who considered Enid her special charge, her refugee, clutched the young woman's arm and pointed at the window displays. She named items that caught her eye—*lamp, teapot, men's shoes*—articulating carefully, as if for a toddler. Rose trailed behind.

They crossed the street and arrived at a corner florist's. "Lilies!" Fiona cried. She released Enid and hurried to the door.

Enid gave Rose a questioning glance.

"We have lots of time," Rose said. "I'll wait out here."

She texted Lloyd to remind him to pick up the marquee bulbs on his way in. She Googled *Toronto weather*, a habit she'd been unable to break despite all the thunderstorms that had come and gone without an episode. *Clouds moving in after 6:00 PM*, she read, *a 10% chance of rain over the next 12 hours.*

A baby carriage entered her side vision, and stopped. She noted the red light. She looked down at the child, a girl (pink tuque), not a newborn but not a toddler either, wrapped tightly in a bunny-patterned blanket and gnawing at her fist. "Oh, how cute," Rose said. She looked at the mother. The mother smiled.

Piano wires snapped in Rose's head. Harriet bent over the child and nudged the pacifier between her lips. She straightened, gave Rose a neutral look that might have been dawning recognition, and pushed the carriage.

Rose blindly followed. A truck turning right almost hit her, and she staggered back and peered above the cars to keep Harriet's small figure in view. Her heart was suffocating. The infant soul she had privately mourned and paired with Ava in eternity was alive. A girl. Could it be that she had gotten through to Harriet, that Harriet had broken under her appeals and commands?

"Rose," said Enid.

Rose turned. She saw Enid as if through etched glass.

"Fiona wants to buy some flowers," Enid said. "Is that okay?"

"Sure," said Rose and followed her into the store.

ACKNOWLEDGMENTS

I am forever indebted to my Canadian publisher, Iris Tupholme, to my agent, Jackie Kaiser, and to my editors, Patrick Crean and Meg Storey. Thanks also to my readers, Marni Jackson, Susan Swan, and Christopher Dewdney, and to repertory-cinema experts Mike Blakesley and Andy Willicks.